THE COWGIRL CHASES THE ROBBERS

COWGIRL MYSTERIES, BOOK 3

SUSAN LOWER

Go get'm girl!

THE COWGIRL CHASES THE ROBBERS

1

If spring has brought anything to Deadwood, it's grey skies and blistery winds. It's unusual for this time of year. The mountain groans in the distance, sending its rumbling sounds through the gulch. It knows what's coming, and like me, it must brace for the impact.

The railroad is coming. The bounty hunter has convinced me there is no stopping it. And in doing so, I've given my permission to allow them to trek across my hard-earned claim in the mountains. There is more than me at stake. Tail Feathers and his people's safety weigh heavily on my shoulders. If the Calvary finds them off the reservation, a war will break out.

By the caterwauling coming down the street, I'd say a war might be right around the bend. For the past week, the bounty hunter and I have been up in the Black Hills talking to the natives and smoothing out the details of keeping the peace. My brown and white paint pony, Lulu, breaks out in a sweat as we ride back into town. My husband, the bounty hunter, tells me to wait outside the sheriff's office for him while he has a word with the man who wears the star.

As I leave Lulu tied in front of the sheriff's office, I go for a walk along with the others to see what the fuss is all about.

Part of me thinks I should stay with Lulu. It's been a hard couple of days on the trial. Not wanting to return, I tried to convince the bounty hunter to let me stay. He threatened to tie me to my saddle despite my childhood friend, Chitto, a brave in Tail Feather's tribe, claiming he would look after me. If I didn't know better, I'd think the bounty hunter was jealous.

No matter, in a few weeks, the bounty hunter assured me we'd go back. I spoke with Chitto and his cousin Yellow Cat, who agreed to help scout the trail for the rail line to come through. I warned Tail Feathers to stay at Standing Rock and away from the rail workers.

With this weather, it will take several weeks, if not months, to dig their way through the mountain.

In the meantime, the bounty hunter insisted we return to Deadwood. I'm not in town five minutes and trouble stirs. My bones ache with the darkening of the clouds. There is no way I'm getting stuck having to stay in this town again.

First, I had to find my father's killer. Then Mr. Conway, the railroad man, offered me a reward to catch the person who framed him for killing one of his own railroad scouts. While my father near cost me our mine claim, the reward from Conway helped me secure it back in my name. Well, my name and the bounty hunter's seeing we're now hitched. At least for the time being, I'm not sure the gambler has it in his mind to give up on proving the bounty hunter and I are anything but married in name only. The bounty hunter's idea, not mine.

But the bounty hunter has got his secrets, and he's not too thrilled to have another wife, so I'll take him as I can get him, and pray one day he'll look at me with more interest than he does his horse.

It won't be long before he comes riding down the street. I decide to let him settle our tab with Hank at the stables while I return my things to the boarding house. Ruby's boarding house has become my home these past couple of months. I promised the bounty hunter I'd meet him at the sheriff's office.

But outside the saloon, I spot all too familiar faces. After years of thinking my mother was dead or worse, she came back to Deadwood looking to get her piece of my father's claim. Thanks to the judge, she got nothing, and rightly so. As did my father's favorite dancing girl, Amaryllis.

Polly Dean screams up a storm in front of the saloon. The sleeve of my mother's dress tears as two men grab at her and Amaryllis trying to keep them from scratching each other's eyes out.

Shoving my way through the crowd, I elbow a fellow to make room for me. I've got enough hip to keep him in line. Right in the middle of things stands the gambler. I should have known I'd find him amid all this.

"Now ladies!" Sheriff Bentely tries to smooth things over and keep the peace. "I'm sure we can work something out."

"Work things out!" Polly sputters, trying to yank out of the sheriff's grasp. "This here is my place! I have an agreement with the bank."

On the other side is Amaryllis, hair falling over her eyes as she grasps Buck Dawson's arm and kicks up her legs to get loose. "Tossed your skirts up for him, you mean! I was here first! This place is mine!"

"Don't matter. You're coming back home with me." Buck keeps his arms around Amaryllis. He's not as tall as most men, but he has broad shoulders and a good head attached to them, but not enough sense to step away while he can.

"No, I ain't!" Amaryllis yells. "You think I'm going back to that ranch to cook and clean my hands to the bone? You're crazy!" She turns on him, holds up her hands. "I'm staying right here at the saloon. Glen and I were partners, and I'm taking over!"

"I'm taking over!" Polly jabs a finger at her chest. "This is my place. You tell her," Polly huffs, looking directly at one flustered banker, Mr. Campbell Reed.

Sheriff Bentely keeps a hand on Polly. "Care to help clear this up?"

Reed clears his throat. He scratches one of his sideburns, looking uneasy. He speaks loud enough for the entire crowd to hear him when he says, "I'd be more than glad to help you, Sheriff, but isn't this more of a domestic dispute?"

Polly's brows knit together as her eyes narrow. Amaryllis has stopped shoving and kicking at Buck. Both women look perturbed enough to hang Reed by his ankles and drag him through the streets, and they might yet, as the gambler puts on his dazzling smile. He spots me and winks, grabbing his lapels and boosting out his chest. "Perhaps it is best I do, Sheriff." The gambler glances around, waiting to catch the attention of all the folk.

Behind me, I catch the scent of sweet tobacco. Glancing over my shoulder, my eyes meet those of the bounty hunter. My stomach tightens in a nervous kind of way. He has a way of making my insides melt.

On the other hand, with the way the gambler still has me locked in his view, my stomach twist at the same time. Surely, by now, he would have given up trying to have my marriage to the bounty hunter annulled. Even so, those dimples he displays when he grins has their way with me. I'll never understand why. I'm a married woman.

Behind me, a warm hand presses against my jacket and I find a broad chest against my back. "What's going on?"

I lean my head back. "We're about to find out."

"Now ladies, there's no need to fight. I'm the new owner of the saloon," the gambler announces.

All eyes turn to the banker. Reed confirms it. "Sorry ladies, Mr. Weston purchased the property outright."

Polly and Amaryllis both explode in a riot of screams and flying limbs. Their target isn't the gambler. They're both headed toward each other, with Reed unable to escape in the middle of it fast enough.

"I'm going to kill you!" Polly screams. "This is my place. We had a deal!"

"A deal perhaps," Reed steps back as the sheriff snatches Polly a breath from scratching his eyes out. Buck has Amaryllis around the waist. Her cheeks are red as her dress. "Mr. Weston here had the cash, my dear. I'm sure you understand it's purely business."

Out of the corner of my eye, I catch sight of a man in a torn Calvary jacket. He ducks his head and grabs his horse. I elbow the bounty hunter. His slate-grey eyes look at me in question. I tilt my chin toward the man, but he's gone.

"That's right," the gambler beams with pride. "You did a fine job cleaning it up for me," the gambler grins wider at Polly. "And you're welcome to come work for me." He winks at Amaryllis, shying away as Buck glowers.

Amaryllis gasps. Her anger goes south and big fat tears well in the woman's eyes.

As the crowd gets bored with the entertainment, they disburse. Trying to keep their attention, the gambler shouts, "You all come back this evening, you hear? The Weston Gambling House will be open for business!"

Why doesn't this surprise me?

Polly wretches free of the sheriff, and while she and Amaryllis are about to lay into the gambler, a shot rings out down the street. The sheriff glances at the bounty hunter and as they both take off running, more shots ring out. Shouts come from down the street. "The bank is being robbed! The bank is being robbed!"

Reed takes off like a bullet whizzing down the street. Several riders gallop past, and Buck shoves Amaryllis inside the saloon. The gambler runs in, and Polly lands flat on her stomach. My heart plummets. I dive for Polly as the commotion goes past.

It happens in such a hurry, it takes me a moment to realize the riders are gone, the shooting has stopped, and I lay atop my estranged mother when I should have taken cover inside.

"Oh, Honey Buns, you do care!" Polly exclaims from beneath me. Immediately, I jump off her. I wore my split skirt and my warm jacket, knowing we'd be riding out of town today. There is no way I want it soiled by the likes of Polly Dean. She may have given birth to me, but the woman abandoned me and my father in the mountains when I was a child. She's no mother to me.

Deep down, mother or no mother, doesn't mean I want anything to happen to her. Which is why when relief floods my system, I'm okay with it. No one's dead.

"Someone get the doctor! Campbell Reed has been shot."

Oh, dear lord, here we go again!

"You fools! Stop trying to kill me and get back my money!" Campbell Reed bellows from where he lies on the boardwalk a few feet from the bank. He's propped up against the wall below the bank window, cracked and littered with holes from the shootout.

Not far across from him lays Sheriff Bentely.

"You'll live. Bring him to my place so I can patch that hole in his shoulder." Doc Chierhat calls going over to the sheriff. He's an older man with a set of steady hands and a little house a few streets over from Main. Cheirhat grimaces at the sheriff. My stomach turns sour making me nauseas. If the sheriff is laying here shot, what happened to the bounty hunter?

Last I saw my husband, he took off with the sheriff. "Where's the bounty hunter? Where's Chord?" I ask.

Deputy Payne keeps pressure on the sheriff's chest. The doctor gets down beside him, and there's too much blood to determine if he'll live or not. Several men help pick up Sheriff Bentely. "Don't know if he'll make it back to my place. That bullet is too close to his heart," Doc Chierhat says.

"Then take him to the boarding house," I say. "Ruby will give him a room and if need be, he can have mine." I won't be needing it. If I know anything about my husband, the bounty hunter, is he'll want to give chase, and I'm going with him.

While visiting my claim on the mountain, we stopped by the railroad camp and met the new foreman. Mr. Conway rode along with us to make plans for the railroad to move ahead. I can't say I blame him for not trusting the job to anyone else after his last foreman betrayed him.

Plus, we needed to make sure Tail Feathers and his tribe were safe. As long as the railroad doesn't go trying to pull one over on our deal to go through the mountain across my land, all should be good while I'm away.

Then it hits me as hard as any bullet. The railroad paid me to use my land, and those robbers just took all the money in the bank — mine included.

I rush with the men carrying the sheriff to the boarding house, questioning again about the bounty hunter's where abouts. The sheriff groans as they move him, but he says, "He took off after those robbers with Buck and some others on his tail."

Nobody bothers knocking at the door of the boarding house. Ruby rushes down the hall toward us. She's got her hair pulled back and tied today, but her face turns white as a sheet at the sight of Sheriff Bentely. The doctor orders them to get him down on a place he can work. Doc barks out a list of what he needs as they lay the sheriff on the dining room table. Ruby stands near him with her hands over her mouth.

"What you waiting for, woman? The sheriff to die?" An ornery cowboy shocks Ruby into motion.

"What about Reed?" someone asks. "He got shot, too."

"Reed can wait," says the doctor. "My wife can tend to him. He's got a scratch compared to this."

I press my hand to my heart to keep it from bursting out of my chest. Slowly, I back out of the room, as the doctor declares for us to clear out while he works.

Spotting Deputy Payne coming through the doorway, I ask. "Any idea which way they went?"

"Nope," Deputy Payne shrugs. "I came to check on the sheriff."

By the look on his face, I'm not all that convinced he is telling the truth.

"The bullet is near his heart."

Deputy Payne turns on his heel. "If you'll excuse me, with the sheriff otherwise detained. It's up to me to see to the safety of the folks in this town."

I cross my arms and keep him from going around me. "Shouldn't you be out there going after the robbers?"

"Somebody's got to stay in town and take care of things." He rests his hand on the butt of his gun.

When I don't move, he rolls back his shoulders. "I seem to remember a time when I had you locked up in jail. Need I do it again?"

I got locked in jail on purpose. How else could I gather information to help find who murdered the railroad scout? While I was in there, Deputy Payne had a visitor. A wanted man, whose face graces the poster outside the sheriff's office. I think better than to bring it up. Instead, I step aside and let the deputy go about his business.

As he leaves, the gambler comes through the door. He takes

me by the shoulders and in those emerald green eyes of his; I see the worry evaporate. What would make the gambler worry about me?

Right before my father died, the gambler beat him in a card game. He won me, and part of our mining claim in the mountains. While he may have gotten his share of the mining claim, he didn't get me. The judge married me to the bounty hunter, Chord Townes. Thanks to Ruby's testimony from over at the boarding house, the judge deemed it necessary. I swear there was nothing more between us than some lace pulling. How else would I get into that corset he bought me? Yeah, he bought me a dress, after mine got destroyed by my father's killer, Glen, the old owner of the saloon. Now the saloon belongs to the gambler. He invested the reward money I used to buy back my father's share of our claim in a gambling hall. Not my money. Not anymore. The gambler can spend his share anyway he wants.

Wait until Reverend Carter gets wind of this. Shaking my head, I try not to chuckle at the thought of Reverend Carter giving the gambler a private sermon.

"I'm glad to see you're safe, darlin'," I hear the sincerity in his voice. "Any news on the sheriff?"

"The doc's got him on the table," I say.

The gambler takes me by the arm and pulls me over to the parlor. Guests scatter about the house after the news of the robbery, but the parlor is empty.

"I wanted to let you know I'm here for you, darlin'. Nothing changes. I heard how the bounty hunter ran out on you. The judge will come back around. We can get the marriage annulled. I've got plenty of room at the gambling house, a private room where you never have to worry about being taken care of."

I had hoped in the time away with the bounty hunter in the mountains, the gambler would have given up pursuit. He got his money. Why would he still possibly want to marry me?

"No worries. I can take care of myself." I say, "Even if my husband isn't around." Being sure to point out the married part.

Right now, it's the bounty hunter who worries me. Call me crazy. The man hunts outlaws for money for a living, but deep inside I'm trembling with thoughts of him getting shot. Our relationship might be a business only kind of thing. Or it was until he kissed me a few weeks back. A girl can dream, can't she?

Our brief trip to my claim on the mountain should have given folks the impression we were on a newlywed getaway. Had the gambler been too busy buying the saloon to notice? He's a sly one. I don't doubt he's always up to something.

"With the bank being robbed, and all the money stole, all you got left is that pretty pony tied down in the livery stables."

My 'pretty pony' as he refers to my paint mare, is the one he tried to sell when he thought he could get away with marrying me and taking over my assets.

He takes my silence as an opportunity to keep talking. "Figured it was a matter of time before a man like Townes would take off on the run again."

"He's not on the run. He's chasing after the robbers."

"What are you going to do until he comes back? *If* he comes back?" The gambler places a hand on my arm. Glancing at his hand, my fist aches with the memory of the last time I slugged him. Maybe he remembers, too, because he pulls away, almost afraid.

"He'll come back, and when he does, he'll have a new bounty over the back of his saddle," I say.

"And no money in the bank to pay." The gambler looks entirely too happy.

"Jo?" Ruby comes into the room. "I hate to ask, but can

you make up the cot in the back room near the kitchen? The sheriff isn't going to be able to go far until he has more time to heal."

"He'll live?" I turn away from the gambler, grateful to have an excuse to get away from him.

"We'll see. It'll be touch and go for a while." Ruby wrings her hands in her skirt. "It could have been worse. Poor Mr. Reed got shot too, and they knocked poor Sherman clean out. "

I can't believe it.

"He took a job for Mr. Reed at the bank. He figured it was safer than the hotel."

Poor guy, always in the wrong place at the wrong time. Sherman worked for the hotel until Daphne and I went down the stairs in an unfortunate event which left Sherman lying flat out cold in the foyer. If anyone should hold a grudge against me, it should be Sherman.

While the sheriff may survive, and Reed will live another day, my money and my husband may have become a fleeting memory.

Looks like I'm going to have to do some tracking on my own. Watch out bad guys, Jolene Willow Dean wants her money back.

2

I promise Ruby I'll help, at least for tonight. There's no sense in taking off until the sun rises again to catch up with my husband. Together, I know we'll find the robbers and get my, and the town's, money back.

But ever since the gambler put doubts in my head, I can't get them out. What if the bounty hunter took this as his opportunity to ditch me and go off on his own again? It's not like we got hitched for a love match or anything.

Maybe he figured he was securing his investment after I offered a piece of my claim to help hunt down my father's killer. Or maybe he didn't want to see me tied down against my will to the gambler. Either way, the bounty hunter never asked me to be his wife. He doesn't whisper sweet nothings in my ear or pull me tight into his embrace at night. The entire week we spent in the mountains, we slept in separate bedrolls.

Come sunrise, I'm going to hunt down a bunch of thieves. They could have killed someone during their thieving. I may not have been one of Sherman's favorite people, but he didn't deserve another head injury.

This time, he can't blame me since I did land on him after

falling down a flight of stairs in the hotel recently. It caused a giant goose egg on his head.

If it's not one thing in this town, it's another.

While Ruby fusses over the sheriff to get him settled, I go for a walk. I end up at the stables to check on Lulu, my paint pony. Someone has taken off her saddle and brushed her down. She's beat from the journey. Her ears are down flat and her eyes hooded in sleep. I don't touch her in fear of startling the dear beast. Content to find her safe and well cared for, I walk back to the boarding house. By now, Ruby should have finished getting the sheriff situated.

As night tries to slip across the sky, Hank offers to walk me back to the boarding house. His wife made fresh pies earlier in the day and sends one along with him for the sheriff. Sweet baked apple is a great weakness of mine. My mouth salivates as I carry it.

Hank doesn't come in. In this cooler air for the beginning of June, the man doesn't wear sleeves. Those bulging muscles in his arms are the envy of every man and the flustration of every woman in town. And yes, *flustration*, not frustration, because what girl can resist a set of powerful arms like Hanks? His wife is one lucky woman.

The lamp glows inside the saloon. Sounds of a piano float down the street. The gambler has wasted no time in opening his new place. Thankfully, Hank's big body blocks the view as we pass. It's none of my business where Polly landed or if Amaryllis is back dancing inside. She and Buck have been in rocky territory since the May Festival a couple weeks back.

I guess it's true what they say. You can take the dance hall girl out of the saloon, but she'll still sing for her supper.

Back at the boarding house, I head for the kitchen. Shedding my coat and grabbing an apron, I pick up a knife and chop carrots. Ruby fusses over the sheriff for the hundredth time. She's got it bad for the man, but will never admit it. A widow, she never remarried or had kids of her own.

Between the two of us, we put together a vegetable stew and I whip up the biscuits.

One good thing about the gambler's new investment, he moved out of the boarding house earlier in the day.

There are six of us for supper, minus Ruby, who tries to get some broth into the sheriff.

Mr. Clark, another boarder, assists me in cleaning up and doing the dishes. He takes coffee out to the others, and we slice up the pie from Hank's wife.

Hearing someone come back into the kitchen, I ask them to help dry the plates piling up. Without a word, they pick up the drying cloth, take the plate from me, and the tingling sensation from their fingers to mine startles me.

"No need to get jumpy, Dimples. Unless you ask every man to dry your dishes." The humor in his voice does little to stop my heart from thundering.

I nearly drop the next plate. "You're back."

"Worried?" He takes the plate before I drop it.

"I didn't think you'd be back. Weren't you chasing the robbers?"

"I don't chase." The way he says it sends tiny spirals of tingles under my skin.

"You're a bounty hunter." I finish the last plate and turn to him.

Those cold stone eyes show some surprise. "Never thought I'd see you going domesticated on me."

I snort, cover my nose and mouth with my hand, shocked at making the sound.

The corner of his tight lips lift. The bounty hunter is made of rock. Seldom have I ever heard him laugh or seen him smile. Although my eyes fall to those tight lips of his and remember a time not too long ago, they sent heat spiraling under my skin with a kiss that could melt a snow-capped mountain.

While I wouldn't want to face the man on the street or play a game of cards with him, I wouldn't mind a repeat of our kiss.

But I see the weariness on his face, the lines on his brow, and the coldness in his eyes. He came back here for a reason. As much as I'd like to think he came back for me, he puts the dried plate away and hooks those thumbs in this gun belt.

"Chord," Ruby steps out of the little room off the kitchen where the sheriff rests. "Joe's been asking for you to see him when you got back."

I walk into the dining room, grab the empty coffeepot, and fill it with more water. While it heats, I warm the vegetable soup I saved for Ruby. "You should get some rest. The bounty hunter is with him, and I'll check on him."

Ruby can't fool me. I've seen the way she fusses over the sheriff.

"You have done enough for the night." Ruby tries to wave me away.

Once the soup is warm, I push it her way. "Don't get used to it."

Faintly, she smiles, and it warms my heart to know I've earned her approval. Having not grown up with my mother, Ruby, and my best friend, Ella Mae's mother, Pearl, filled the empty spot inside me. Not that it took two women to do the work of one. Oh no, Polly Dean took off and left me. She wasn't then, and she isn't now, mother material.

Having Pearl teach me a thing or two and Ruby watch after me when my father brought us to town was a pure blessing. The least I can do is try to return Ruby's kindness. As far as I know, she doesn't have any kids of her own.

"I should see to cleaning up the dining room. I think Mrs. Miller asked for an extra blanket tonight. Perhaps Reverend

Carter knew something when he warned us our sins would change the weather."

"I believe he said hell would freeze over, or was it we'd all burn?" Either way, Mother Nature hadn't gotten the memo. Things were supposed to get hotter around here, but at the moment they were frigid.

"I should get that blanket," Ruby says, wistfully for the second time.

"Sit." I command. "Eat the soup and watch the coffee pot. I'll grab the blanket, then when I get back to bed with you. For a nap." I know I can't get her to sleep longer. I can't. My mind has been reeling with the day's events.

"The dining room is done, and the dishes are finished. Sit." I point again at a chair. Ruby pouts, but does as I tell her.

I know where the blankets are. Grab one and deliver it to the Miller's room. Tonight is their first night at the boarding house.

Back in the kitchen, the coffee brews and I send Ruby up the stairs for some shuteye. She's worse than a stubborn mule, afraid of the rushing current of the river to take to water.

Coffee done. Ruby in her room. I pour a cup, adding sugar, and lean against the doorjamb to the little side room Ruby calls her pantry. I don't mean to eavesdrop. Just the opposite. I stay back, not wanting to interfere.

The bounty hunter sits in a chair by the cot where the sheriff rests. He shed his duster and holds his hat. His head bent low. I can hear the soft murmur from the sheriff. The bounty hunter's back stiffens and I take it as my cue to slip in and hand him a cup of coffee. Lightly touching his arm, he glances over at me. Seeing the coffee, he curls his fingers around the cup and gives me a nod.

I may or may not have put a little more sugar in it than he normally takes. A girl can try to sweeten up a man, can't she?

"Did you find them?" Sheriff Bentely asks.

"Buck's leading a posse. They're headed toward Silver Valley."

"You don't think they'll go that way?" Sheriff Bently asks.

"No. They'll need to lie low. My guess is they have a place."

"You came back."

"I needed to grab supplies and a guide." The bounty hunter looks right at me.

"Me?"

He shakes his head. "Sorry, Dimples. I don't doubt you know those mountains, but I believe you have a friend who can help."

Chitto. For the first time in my life, I'm jealous of my old-time friend, and first love. Introducing the bounty hunter to Chitto may not have been the best idea. Chitto once offered my father two ponies for my hand in marriage. I've still got Lulu, and the bounty hunter gave back the other pony a few weeks back. Chitto still considers me his. Would the bounty hunter and Chitto go into the fight circle over me?

"You tracked them to the mountains?" Sheriff Bently eases his hand under the blanket Ruby tucked him in.

"No, but if I were them, I would hide there."

The sheriff seems to consider the bounty hunter's words. He curls his hand around something and drags it out.

The bounty hunter puts his hand over the man's arm before he can show it. "No."

"You're the best man for the job."

The bounty hunter's eyes go cold, almost dull as thick ice. Tension radiates through his body, filling the small space around the three of us.

"Which is why I'm going after him. There's a bounty on them. I don't need a badge to bring them in."

My eyes widened. The sheriff blinks, his eyes dropping. Probably from the drugs the doctor gave him to ease the pain and sleep.

I chew on my lip, trying not to interfere, but can't help blurting out, "Shouldn't you let the deputy handle things for you until you're well?"

Both men look at me as if I tossed a dead fish in their laps.

"He'll try, but the kid is too green," Sheriff Bently implores the bounty hunter once more. "You've been tracking him for years. Take the star, Chord. You're the only man I trust with the job. I need you. This town needs you." Bently whispers, he coughs, blood trickling down his lip.

Fear spikes within me. Hurriedly, I grab the edge of the blanket and dab away the blood. Never mind, I'm hanging over the bounty hunter like yesterday's laundry waiting to dry.

"Deputy Payne will do fine until you are on your feet again," the bounty hunter says.

The sheriff's hand shakes trying to hand the gold star to the bounty hunter. I help him, pressing it into Chord's palm. He looks as if he swallowed a frog at contact.

"Think about it. All I'm asking." The sheriff's eyes drift shut, and I tug on the bounty hunter's arm. He's got a half cup of coffee in one hand and a golden star in the other.

Back in the kitchen, I plate him the last piece of Hank's wife's pie, the one I saved for myself.

While he eats, I tell him. "The bullet slid near his heart. Couldn't move him upstairs. Can't move him too much until he heals. Doc wasn't sure the bullet nicked nothing vital. There wasn't an exit in the back."

The bounty hunter nods, slowly, understanding. I offer to refill his coffee, but he puts his hand over the top of the mug. "I know what you're thinking Dimples, don't."

"You were a Texas Ranger, right? What difference would it be to fill in for the sheriff while he's down? Ain't like he's asking you to do it forever. He said you've been tracking him. Why?"

There's something personal about this outlaw. I can feel it as sure as I can see I've hit a nerve.

The fork clatters against the plate. I grab his hand before he can take off. We've been here, done this before, once in a cafe over the same kind of pie. "I ain't asking anything about your past or your secrets, as is our deal," I say. "You think if you're sheriff you can't get the bounty on the Brownell gang? Is that it?"

"No." He yanks his hand back from me, tossing the star from the other hand beside the plate. "The Texas Rangers was a long time ago. Me and the law don't side together."

My stomach sours. "You want to kill him, don't you?"

His face hardens and I know I'll get no more out of him. But it's something. More than something. For the first time in weeks, he slips and lets me see a little a part of him he likes to keep hidden.

"One of them did you wrong. I get that." I reach across him and snatch the gold star. Ever since my father was killed and almost losing my claim, I've had a strong sense of justice. "You don't want to fill in for the sheriff, I will. Don't make me arrest you."

He gives me a quizzical look.

"What?" I shrug. "Can't do a worse job than if Payne takes over as the sheriff. Besides, a girl has to make a living somehow. Those Brownell outlaws took all my money and most of the towns."

He finishes his coffee, stands, rolling back his shoulders. He doesn't intimidate me. The opposite, in fact. Seeing him stand up in front of me, the gun holstered at his hip, and those thumbs hooking into his belt loops. He tilts up his chin. A day's worth of growth on his cheek sends reminders of when his lips pressed on mine. It makes my heart leap with anticipation. It seems like forever ago.

Those cold stone eyes of his harden their gaze. "No, you won't. Get it out of your head right now, Dimples."

"Watch me." I move to pin the star on my blouse when the bounty hunter curls his hand around mine, holding the star.

There is a battle in those eyes. His thumb rubs my knuckles, sending ripples of sensation up my arm.

For a second, I wonder where he has gone. He's looking at me, but I can tell his mind has taken him somewhere. I give him a minute, swallowing back everything in my head, wanting to be said. His lips fall, the lines on his forehead deepen. Unable to resist, I reach up with my free hand, press my hand to the side of his face. It makes him tilt his face into my touch, his eyes close for a moment, and when he opens them, he steps back out of my reach with the star in his hand.

I'm left feeling empty in more ways than one.

"Go to bed Dimples. I'll stay up with Bentely until Ruby comes to check on him."

"You should go to our room. Get some sleep. Think about what you're going to do." I hitch my chin in the direction of the gold star.

"I don't have to think about it." He turns it in his hand, between his fingers, weighing it and the decision he made.

"You should rest."

"I'll get it when I need it. Don't worry about me, Dimples."

Why do those words not ease my concerns? I shouldn't worry about a man who hunts outlaws for a living. Something unspeakable must have happened for him to walk away from the law.

Now, he's more dangerous than a snake under a rock.

But so are the Brownell brothers and their gang. Why else would they all have a price on their heads? Why else would the bounty hunter continue to track him?

3

Ruby doesn't have to wake me the next morning. I've been awake for hours, ready to go. The only thing holding me back has been the dark. I can't go breaking into Hank's livery stables to get Lulu until sunrise. Hank's a smart man, he keeps his stables protected and I'm not about to kiss the end of his hot iron or test the temperature of his forge. The man may have arms of steel, but he doesn't take to people trespassing on his livelihood, good reason or not.

There's coffee. The scent is intoxicating. There's always coffee, but this morning the fare is simple. Porridge. No one dares complain. As I glance around the corner, Ruby is with Sheriff Bently. I think she's aged ten years from one man's gunshot wound.

For a moment I wonder what I would do if the tables turned, if the bounty hunter lie in the sheriff's place, and my heart squeezes. We haven't known each other long, but I've grown attached.

"Have you seen the bounty hunter?"

"I'm sorry, Jo. He's gone."

"Gone?" My throat goes dry, and I croak the word.

"Headed to gather his horse, I imagine." There are dark circles around Ruby's eyes. I wish I could stay to help her. As much as I feel duty bound to remain here and help, another part of me knows I have to go. There is no way I'm allowing the bounty hunter to leave me behind. Good thing I left my coat hanging in the kitchen. You'd think for June a girl wouldn't need a jacket, but the mornings are cool, and the days don't warm like they did last summer.

I take off down the hall to run into a stumbling gambler. He's not coming down the stairs, he's headed inside. "Jolene, darlin'! You're just the woman I want to see."

I don't have the time to stop and chat, not if I'm going to catch up with the bounty hunter. "I figured you moved over into that sin house of yours."

He laughs, those adorable dimples of his coming out this early in the morning. "Can't a man invite a woman to breakfast?"

"I'm married," I call as I flee past. "Best you move on and find another."

Even as I put more distance between us, the thought of him with another woman rolls my stomach over. I happen to know Miss Davenport hasn't given up her dreams of snagging him into marriage before her betrothed comes to collect her.

The gambler got his money, and he's got his fancy new saloon for gambling, girls, and firewater. The entire town is going to freeze over soon from the sin spreading faster than a wildfire.

A sweat builds between my shoulder blades, soaking the back of my blouse, sticking it to my jacket. Running the last stretch to the opening of the stables, I skid to a halt. My heart pounding. Searching frantically, I swipe the moisture from my forehead.

Hank steps out of a small room, wiping his hands. For

once, the man has a shirt on, cuffs rolled up on his forearms. His forge is fired, and the iron waits to get heated.

"Where is he?" I pant, trying to get my lungs to catch up with me.

Hank shrugs.

"His horse? Where is the bounty hunter's horse?"

Hank looks beyond me.

"You hanging out with the gambler again, Dimples? I might have given you my name, but a man has to draw a line somewhere."

A smile creeps its way across my lips. I spin on my heel and do what any wife would do. I cross my arms and give him the most furious scowl I can. "Where do you think you're going?"

"It's too early in the morning for a fight." The bounty hunter holds the reins of his horse in one hand and pushes back the side of his duster to reveal his six-shooter with the other.

My gaze follows the movement. I should have known a man like him would turn on me. Good thing I have Shorty packed with my belongings. A girl should never go anywhere without a little fire power. As I try to pull Shorty from my pack, the gun gets caught on a strap.

"You tried to give me the slip." I grimace, cussing under my breath as I can't get Shorty out.

"I told you to stay at the boarding house." He rests his hand on the butt of his gun.

Yanking and tugging, I'm about to scream. I can't get Shorty to budge. "No." I say between gritted teeth. "I told you I was going after the bounty."

The bounty hunter lays a hand on his horse's neck, patting it. "You're going to get yourself hurt."

"Why? You gonna shoot me? Because that's the only way you're gonna keep me from going after those robbers."

The bounty hunter drops the reins of his horse. "Stay." He

commands the horse. The roan stallion doesn't move as the bounty hunter approaches. Crouching down, he grabs the strap on the pack and Shorty slides out. "Those men are more than robbers, Jo."

He rarely calls me Jo. "I know. They shot the sheriff, Reed, and hurt poor Sherman. We have to go after them. We both know Buck and the others won't catch up to them. But you can."

"I can get to them faster on my own. I appreciate you coming to see me off, Dimples, but they've got a good lead already. Unless you came to give me directions to find that scout who can help me." There is steel in his eyes, and if I were any other right-minded woman, I would back down and run from the look in his eye alone. But I don't. I'm not afraid of him. I should be, I know. He's a man killer, a hunter of outlaws, and a man of many secrets. But I can't help the attraction I feel for him. He makes my skin tingle in a bunch of good ways and the man hasn't ever laid a hand on me.

There is no way I'm letting him go anywhere without me. During our time in the mountains, Chitto found us at the shack my father called a cabin. I'm not about to give the bounty hunter directions to ride straight into Tail Feather's camp. He would be crazy to go there alone.

I glance back over my shoulder. Hank puffs air into his forge to make it hotter.

"The only way you're finding Chitto is by taking me," I say, glad Hank is far enough away not to hear us.

"I didn't come back for you Dimples. I need you here, helping Ruby and watching over the sheriff."

"Why?"

"We both know Payne is worthless."

"I don't trust him." It's the truth. I saw him a while ago talking with one of the Brownell brothers, Brody. Now that I think of it, maybe the deputy was in on the robbery. I'd say as much to the bounty hunter, but then a glint on his shirt catches my eye. "You took the badge. You're the sheriff."

Standing, Shorty dangles at my side. "I didn't think you'd do it."

"We won't speak of it; I'll be back to return Bently his badge once I track down the Brownell gang."

"One man can't take down an entire gang. You need my help."

"I need you to stay here." He raises with me, several inches over my height, but I don't miss the jump in his jaw muscle.

"They're headed toward Silver Valley, but I know Brody. He'll circle around and cut up the side of the mountains."

"There are a lot of places, old claims and such to hide out." I play with my braid, tugging on the end in thought. "We'll need Chitto for sure. He knows more of the deer paths than I do." Plus, Chitto is a better tracker than I am, but I won't admit it to the bounty hunter.

"Not *we*, Dimples. Me. You stay here."

I curl my finger around Shorty's trigger. "They stole my money, and I ain't about to get stuck in this town penniless again. I suppose I could go back to my place in the mountains."

"No." The bounty hunter reaches in his pocket, pulls out a wad of greenbacks. He peels out a half dozen and holds them out. "This is more than enough to keep you until I get back."

"Don't make me shoot you."

Quick as a snake strike, he grabs the wrist of my hand holding Shorty. "I'm the last person you want to threaten." His voice holds a deadly edge, one that sends zings up my arm from his touch. My heart takes a leap in my chest. Maybe I am a little afraid of him. After all, I don't know the bounty hunter that well. He's a private man, and we have a deal. I don't pick at his secrets, and he doesn't tell anyone about Tail Feathers and Chitto's tribe living on Standing Rock off the reservation.

Should the Calvary find out, they'll herd them back on the land prison we have forced them to survive on. All my life, my father and I have traded with the natives on the mountain. Without Chitto, my childhood friend, I would not have survived in the wilderness. My mother abandoned me physically, my father emotionally. He lived on firewater and tobacco and occasionally the hard tack and stew I learned to keep us alive on.

I had enough hard tack in my pack to keep me fed for a week. When I didn't take the bounty hunter's money, he huffed and shoved it in my coat pocket. As I went to give it back, he grabbed my other arm. Tilting his head forward, his hat brim collided with mine, tipping mine back off my head. Good thing I keep my hat string around my neck as it slides down my back.

"You're not going."

"Yes I am."

"No."

"Yes."

"Kiss her and go before she comes to her senses again," Hank calls.

He might as well have lit a match against my face as heat flares in my cheeks. The bounty hunter's forehead touches mine. This simple touch causes my breath to hitch.

"Jo." He says it gruff, a warning, but his hands still hold my arms and not his gun.

We're wasting time. My heart beats faster. For a moment, I think he will kiss me. I've waited for an encore from our kiss weeks ago at our wedding feast at the hotel. It was the first time he kissed me, and I prayed it wouldn't be the last. I lick my lips in anticipation. Closing my eyes, I feel his breath against me. His nose glides along the side of mine, but when he talks, his lips have moved closer to my ear. "I hate to do this."

Before I can ask what, suddenly I'm twisted around. Shorty

is yanked from my grasp, and both my hands are behind my back. "What are you doing?"

"Keeping my wife alive." His words send a wave of shock through me. I don't hear the clink of the metal cuffs around my wrist over the roaring of my ears. The cold steel makes me wince.

"Bounty hunter!" Jerking in his grasp, he backs me against one of the stalls. He lifts my arm above my head as I try to fight him. Keeping my other arm locked between us, his lips land hard on mine. Stunned, I freeze, then slowly relax into the softening pressure of his kiss. My eyes flutter closed. Then, as suddenly as it started, the kiss ends.

As I'm whirled around, my eyes fly open. Another clink of the cuffs catches my attention. What warm and fuzzy feelings I had spread through me are doused by the cold splash of trickery.

"I told you." His lips are at my ear again. "Call me Chord. Practice it while I'm gone." Then he releases me. Leaping forward, I'm yanked back by the restriction of the cuffs, causing me to cry out from the metal digging into my wrist.

Chord, the bounty hunter, takes up his reins and walks past me.

"Told you it would work," Hank says, and I shot him with a death glare. On his way, the bounty hunter picks up my pack and my shot gun. He tosses the pack at Hank.

"That's my gun." Twisting and pulling down on my hand, I'm not going anywhere. The bounty hunter has cuffed me to a metal tie ring on the wall. "Don't you dare take it."

If he hears me, the bounty hunter pays me no mind. He leads his horse past Hank and says, "Wait a few hours when she's cooled down and let her go. I've already told Payne to lock her up if she tries to leave town."

"And the pony?" Hank asks.

"I'll pay you extra to make sure it doesn't leave the stables."

"Done." Hank doesn't smile when the bounty hunter disappears from the barn. In his hand lies the key to my freedom.

"Hank," I say.

He shakes his head. "It's for your own good, Jo. A man can't do his job if he thinks his wife is in danger. You won't talk me into letting you go a minute sooner. I'd do the same thing."

Biting my lip, I try to hold back the tears of frustration welling in my eyes. Sliding down the wall, I sit. One arm raised, held by the cuff, I kick out at a dropping of hay.

If the bounty hunter thinks he can keep me from going after the robbers, he's wrong.

Hank goes back to pounding metal on his forge. Lulu is a few stalls away, and my chances of catching up with the bounty hunter, or the robbers, slip away with every strike of Hank's hammer.

I lean my head back, let the dam of tears overflow. All the while on the outside, I may appear a weak, stubborn woman. In my head, I curse the bounty hunter and Hank, all the while planning to catch the Brownell gang on my own.

4

By the time lunch rolls around, my arm has gone numb, and I've gone from three levels of angry, frustrated, and downright vengeful. I can hear Ella Mae in my mind giving me a sweet sermon she most likely heard from her father. Vengeance is for the Lord. Well, God, how do you suppose I get myself out of this one?

I've long closed my eyes, but not given up. I've played every scenario in my mind to get Hank to let me go. Even Layla, Hank's wife, tried to plead my case. He's a good man. A man of his word.

Oh, how I hate the bounty hunter right now. I hear the clang of Hank's hammer against metal. It eases every once in a while, and I can't image a horse in town without new shoes for all the racket he's been making. A few men have walked through, gathering horses, or bringing new ones in off the trail. Some of them make the hairs in my nose burn as they go by, and that's saying something when you've been sitting by a pile of horse manure for a few hours.

They'll head to Eva and Emma Swanson's for a bath. It's where all the men go to wash off the trail and then some.

I don't open my eyes as I hear someone approach. The sounds of their shoes crunching against the dirt and the hay come to a stop. Even then, I ignore the sound.

"Why look here." I recognize his voice. It's Deputy Payne. I try to ignore him. He's probably not looking at me. Then a hand touches my chin and my eyes open. No such luck. The wet-behind-the-ears deputy grins. "Suppose I should take you in and lock you up. I won't have to chase you later."

"Chord said to let her go after lunch." Hank walks toward us, sweat trickling down the side of his face.

"Go on then, let her go. We both know she's trouble. I got more important things to do than chase some other man's wife."

The doubt in Hank's eyes says he's sorry as his gaze meets mine.

"Well, go on. You forget who the law is here in town?"

"Sheriff Bentely?" I ask.

Payne's eyes narrow. "He gave up his badge. Man can't chase outlaws if he's six feet under."

"He's dead?" Panic seizes my chest and all I can think of in this moment is poor Ruby.

"No. And you ain't the only law," Hank corrects Payne. "We got a new Sheriff in town. Townes."

Payne scowls, his nostrils flaring. I notice he's got his gun strapped to his thigh and his trousers don't have a speck of dust on them.

"For now." Payne places his hands on his hips. "But he isn't here right now, is he? So, I'm the one upholding the law, you hear?"

Hank snorts. "We'll see about it. There's still a matter of the robbery and the shooting."

"The bounty hunter will track them and bring them back." There I go again not using his name. My fingers in my raised hand are cold. I know because when Hank clasps his hand on mine, it near burns my fingers from the contact.

"They'll be long gone by now. Suppose it's your fault for him having to return and delaying the chase. No wonder he said to lock you up. Again." He adds, having gotten myself locked up not too long ago so I could talk to a prisoner.

Liam Payne gives me the impression he's as honest as a thief on Sunday. The way his eyes glint with delight at the prospect of locking me up makes me ill. My wrist slips down as Hank releases the cuff around the tie ring. Pain shots up my arm and causes me to groan. The blood all rushes back down the limb and I bite my lip through the awful sensation.

"You can't lock me up. I have done nothing wrong."

"Obstructing justice, or at least that's what Townes told me."

"I thought he said to lock her up if she tried to leave town," Hank says.

"That's Sheriff Townes to you." I grit my teeth again, wiggling my fingers.

"Get up. I got other places I need to go. Bad enough I must be seen looking after a woman." Standing tall, he rests his hands on his gun belt, puffing his chest. Those sandy-blonde locks threatening to cover his eyes.

"You come here for something?" Hank asks.

"Did any of those outlaws' horses come through the livery?" Payne asks.

"Yep. Switched out the two on the end, but Townes had a good look over them earlier. Nothing there to help you."

Payne cups the back of his neck and frowns for a moment. "They didn't leave anything else?"

"Just the horses. Took their own gear."

I watch Hank as the two men speak. He gives me a sympatric smile. Happy to have me out of his stable, Hank hands the key to Payne as the man grabs my cuff and tugs to make me get up.

"You're not going to cuff her to you?" Hank asks.

Payne smirks. "I've got my gun if she tries to run."

My jaw hangs open. I cradle my arm against my stomach, trying to work the blood flow back in enough for the prickling sensation to stop.

"Use it and Townes will have you next on his list," Hank warns.

Payne takes me by the arm and leads me past Hank. "No trying to get away. You run, I shot. I don't play."

Oh, we're going to play. Stepping outside the stables, I glance around to check if anyone is nearby.

Escorted down the street like a common criminal, it doesn't escape my attention Lottie Larson and Hannah Baker are walking our way. I keep my hand behind my back as they pass. Both wear their pretty bonnets and long-sleeved jackets. Hannah gives me a good long glance, and it doesn't help Payne slow down to tip his hat. He puts on a lopsided grin and where he isn't as nearly as attractive as other men in this town, Hannah blushes.

"Ma'am," Payne says as we pass.

"Lovely day, isn't it?" Hannah asks, then stiffens, bringing her shoulders back as she catches my eye. Her blush fading and her chin lifting higher.

"Don't you worry, ma'am, I'm here to keep you safe."

I try not to snort. Even Lottie bursts in a fit of giggles as I keep walking. It takes Payne a moment to notice he's no longer holding onto my arm. I quickly grab the other side of the cuff and pull it up in my sleeve. The last thing I want to do is give the two women a tidbit to gossip.

My escape is short-lived as Daphne Davenport steps out of the hotel. Her black hair is styled in a twist under a lavender bonnet on to match her dress. At her side is Mr. Warner, the hotel manager.

"Sheriff! Sheriff!" She yells as I scowl and try to walk away from her. She launches into me as something momentarily distracts Warner. He glances back at his hotel. Daphne causes me to stumble to the side, and I grab onto her arms to steady myself. The cuff slips from my sleeve. It dangles against her purple one. Those equally lavender eyes of hers land on the shiny end of my cuff, and they brighten.

"Let me go! Oh help!"

"Stay away from her." Warner shoves me away and my back hits the porch post, causing me to groan. Payne catches up, taking hold of my arm. "You alright Miss Davenport?"

"Her?" I yank my arm from him, grab hold of the cuff again, and keep it in my fist. "She's the one who knocked into me, then he pushed me." I glare at Warner.

He tugs at the tie around his collar. "I was protecting Miss Davenport."

"From what?" I huff. "Her pushing me?"

"Oh, Sheriff, I'm so glad you grabbed a hold of her in time. Why, I was so afraid she'd try to hurt me again." Daphne flutters her lashes, directing her gaze toward her busted ankle. She's got a crutch under one arm. She still blames me for injuring her, despite the fact I saved her life.

"Come on, let's go," Payne tries to grab me again.

"Are you well?" Warner asks.

I interrupt and say, "Just fine. The *deputy* here and I were just on our way to attend to some business."

Daphne leans on Mr. Warner. "I knew it was only a matter of time before the Sheriff locked you up. Daddy was right about you."

"That's where you're wrong. The sheriff isn't locking me up. He's out there chasing down the robbers."

"For all we know, you could be in league with them," Daphne says.

"Come Daphne, your father is waiting for us at the station site," Warner offers his arm at her side.

"We'll be out of your way," Payne says.

Daphne may not be far from the truth. Someone could have been in league with the robbers. The more we head to the sheriff's office, the more I get the impression folks are looking at Payne with a higher regard. It puts a burr beneath my skin.

Across the street, the bank windows appear cracked and littered with a few bullet holes. The door remains closed. Reed locked the place up as if there was anything left inside for someone to take. It wouldn't surprise me if the man kept a secret vault somewhere.

"You don't have to do this," I tell Payne. The man walks like a rooster around a hen house. The closer we get to the sheriff's office, the more it becomes clear. Reed waits for us inside. He's not quick enough to mask his surprise. "What's she doing here?"

"Locking her up," Payne shoves me not so kindly into the nearest cell. I've been here a few times before. I hope the bounty hunter doesn't think he can keep me locked up when he doesn't want me getting involved.

My heart sinks for him. Deep down, I truly believe he did this to protect me. And he wouldn't have done that if he didn't care.

Huh, the bounty hunter has a heart in there, after all.

"Good to see you taking your job seriously, Sheriff. It will please Davenport to know the law is on his side."

"He's not locking me up because of Davenport, and he's not our sheriff," I cross my arms as the cell door swings shut.

Reed grunts. He doesn't look any worse from wear after getting shot during the robbery. His skin's a little pale and looks like he might have forgotten to comb his sideburns. A sling wraps around one arm, keeping it snug against his chest.

"Not the sheriff? Bently can't possibly think to fulfill his duties in his condition."

"I'm taking care of it." Payne moves toward Reed, turning his back on me. "You can count on me."

"Bently is still sheriff?" Reed asks.

"Not exactly." Payne cups the back of his neck. Why does this wet-behind-the-ears deputy seem nervous? Maybe he's afraid the lie will catch up with him.

"What is that supposed to mean?" Reed rubs his wounded arm, wincing.

"It means, Mr. Reed, that Chord Townes is the sheriff."

Payne's shoulders stiffened.

"Townes? The bounty hunter?" Reed asks.

"He's an ex-Texas ranger," I add, feeling mighty proud of my man.

"I see." Reed steps back.

I don't think he does.

"Well, I'll leave you to do your duties, *deputy.*" Reed leaves and Payne follows him out, but not before tossing me a dark scowl.

Once he's gone, I heave a sigh of frustration. The bounty hunter is hours ahead of me. The Brownell gang has at least a day's advantage, and here I am left penniless and forced to stay in town again.

Leaning my head forward, my nose touches the cold bars. What's a girl need to do to escape this place?

One thing is for certain, the first chance I get, I'm going to prove to the bounty hunter I can take care of myself. And the best way to do that is to bring in the robbers.

5

"And here the deputy feared giving you a spoon would cause trouble," Ruby's voice rings inside the sheriff's office. "You're gonna wear a tunnel in the floor by all the pacing."

Startled, I whirl around to face her. The scent of her buttered biscuits makes my stomach grumble with recognition of hunger. I've been pacing back and forth in this cell for hours. Payne has come and gone throughout the afternoon.

"How did you know I was here?"

"Chord may have mentioned this morning about instructing Payne to lock you up if you tried to leave town. Can't say I don't agree with him, but as much as I enjoy having you at the house to help me, I don't agree with locking a woman up for wanting to go along with her husband." Ruby sits the plate of biscuits down on the desk and reaches into her apron pocket.

"Oh, he locked me up, but not because I tried to leave. I didn't even get a chance," I huff and tell Ruby the short version of my morning.

"I can't believe I'm doing this." She clucks her tongue, pulling out a set of keys.

"Is that what I think it is?" I grip the bars.

"Complements of Joseph, bless his heart." She smiles wanly, putting the key into the lock.

"What about Payne?"

"He's at the saloon. Seems half the men in town couldn't wait for it to open again. I heard some say Weston has gambling tables and took on a woman partner."

"Partner? Woman. Amaryllis?"

Ruby's lips press together. A sure sign she doesn't want to discuss this anymore. The cell door pops open, and she hands me the key to releasing the cuff still dangling from my wrist.

"I don't want you to get in trouble."

"Not my fault if I came in here and found you gone. I told Chord locking you in jail was a bad idea. Tried to talk him into locking your room door at the house, but he said you'd escape through the window."

"I would." I won't lie. The bounty hunter has snuck in said window a time or two after Ruby has locked up the house for the night.

"Then go. I know I can't talk sense in you. You'll find your horse tied under a tree behind the schoolhouse. Go on." Her eyes water.

"I'm coming back," I hope my words bring her reassurance. "And when I do, I'm bringing those murderous robbers back with me."

"Let Chord chase the robbers, Jo. You've been in enough danger since coming to town. Make a home for your husband when he returns. It's time you and Chord settle down. You both deserve some peace and quiet. Maybe you'll decide to start a family."

I'd like that. The thought of having Chord Townes baby feels pleasant, but nausea creeps up my throat. I don't know if I'm prepared to be a mother. Nor do I think Chord has any ambition to fathering any children, especially by me. He made it clear our marriage is in name only. Even with the gambler trying to prove our marriage is all for show to break our union, the few kisses we've shared have sent heat to parts of me I never knew could burn.

"I don't think my husband wants a home," I confess. Our marriage isn't one of love. Chord Townes is a man of many things. Flowers and heart felt profusions aren't amongst them.

"He might not think so, but the man chose you. He married you." Ruby lays her hand on me. "You'd best go. I don't think anyone will come after you. Payne is too caught up in being the law in town."

"How is the sheriff?" Guilt strikes me. I should have asked first thing.

"He's alive." Ruby's eyes gleam with emotion. "A few prayers couldn't hurt."

Nodding, because I'd do anything for Ruby. And I hoped God would, too. After losing one husband, I don't know if she could stand to lose another man in her life.

"Keep an eye out, would you? I think there's more going on with Deputy Payne. He and Reed are giving me an uneasy feeling." I trust Ruby. She's the mother of my heart. We've talked through finding killers in the past. When my father died, she took me in and allowed me to work off my stay. I don't think she would have turned me out either way.

"Where will you go?" she asks.

"Home," is all I say. The bounty hunter may have left me behind, but I know a man who can give me a leg up in finding the robbers. By the time the bounty hunter searches all the abandoned claims, I'll have beat him back to Deadwood.

Ruby opens her arms and pulls me into a hug. "Be careful." Her support means more to me than she'll ever know.

"Go." She sends me on my way.

Halfway down the street, I hear notes from a piano and laughter floating through the air. Ruby is right. Half the men in town are at the saloon this evening. Light is fading and I don't have much time to get far before night comes.

Curiosity nips at me, and tempting as it is, I can't let those robbers get further away. I owe it to Sherman to bring them to justice. The man never deserved to die by some outlaw thieves. If the bounty hunter is right, Buck and his posse will turn back after Silver Valley. Those kinds of men don't go searching long and give up easy.

The bounty hunter doesn't seem the type to ever let something go. We have a lot in common in this respect.

There will be time later to appease my curiosity. I'm sure Ruby is mistaken, and the gambler has simply employed Amaryllis to work in the saloon again. My mother will have to get over her disappointment at not having the place for herself.

I've never been one to resist the urge of curiosity. One brief look inside won't hurt. The evening has gotten warm, and I shed my jacket. Holding onto it, I approach the saloon. Behind me, I hear the approach of boots. Stiffening, I pause as two cowboys saunter past me. One glances back, tips his hat, and I try not to cringe. He's got a glass eye and a scar so deep south of it I have to resist touching my face.

What once was a small town has been expanding by the day thanks to the news of the Central Railroad coming through.

Walking up to the swinging doors, I spot Deputy Payne leaning against the bar. There are a few men around, but when he turns his head, I duck back.

Maybe this wasn't such a good idea. I peer through the window at the sound of a woman's laugh.

On the other side of the bar, I spot Polly. She's wearing a dark green and black gown. While she pours the next cowboy a drink, she bends close to him. The woman could get rich if she charged for the show. Running my hand down my face, I take a deep breath. In his signature suit stands the gambler. A green vest under his jacket matches Polly's dress. Lord, I hope not. I pinch the bridge of my nose, about to turn away. The deputy has disappeared and my heart thumps in my chest. Where did you go?

Searching around as much as I can through the windows, I spot several other women, one I'm sure is Amaryllis, back in her old habitat.

Swallowing hard, I turn away when a voice sends a ripple of goosebumps across my skin.

"Jolene? Darlin', is that you?"

My shoulders hunch together. I had to go poking my nose where it doesn't belong. Spinning on my boot heel, I greet the gambler. "Quite a place you got here."

Those emerald eyes darken to match the color of his vest. A gold chain dangles from the pocket. "Let me buy you a drink. On the house."

"No thanks." I press my hand to my stomach to calm the nerves. It's not right for a girl to find a man attractive when she's hitched to another.

"Come on now, darlin'. I know you want to come in." He holds out his hand. "I promise to keep you off the table. No bets tonight." He winks.

"You got that right. You've got one Dean in there. You don't need another." I clutch my jacket.

"Oh, don't let that bother you none, darlin'. I couldn't let my future mother-in-law without a means of care."

"Mother-in-law? I've got a husband, and he isn't you."

He grins, dimples and all. If a girl had a weakness, it would be his grin. "For now. You never know what might happen out on the trail. Besides," he wiggles his brows, "the judge will be back soon. We can take your case back in front of him and right the mistake."

"There's no mistake. The bounty hunter is my husband.

You got your money and you've got this place. What you need me for?"

"A man can dream of white picket fences, can't he?" His eyes glint with mischief.

Gold-lined ones, but I keep my thought to myself. Instead, I mutter, "I think Miss Davenport prefers them fancy brick houses."

"A woman of fine quality and taste."

Shocked he heard me, I wave him off. He grabs my hand, and for a moment I allow him to brush his thumb inside my palm. "You're not jealous, are you, darlin'?"

Of Daphne Davenport? Never. "I'm a married woman."

"Keep telling yourself that." His thumb presses into the center of my palm. "Heard Townes took off after those robbers. Someone said he's been tracking the Brownell gang for a long time. Seems a man like him might have a bone to pick. Might find himself dead or on the wrong side of the law."

"What's it matter to you?" I cross my arms, getting defensive. Aware the sun dips lower and my time with it, I have to get on my way.

"You matter to me, darlin'. When Townes doesn't come back, or you tire of waiting, you know where to find me."

He looks beyond me to down the street where the sounds of horses distract him. Four horsemen come trotting towards us. One man holds onto the reins of another horse. Upon its back is a body tied in a blanket.

The gambler places his hand on my arm as he steps in front of me. "You should go get the deputy."

And let him know I escaped? "Pfft." It doesn't take long for the riders to pass us, heading for the sheriff's office. They tie their horses to the rail. Behind us, someone shouts and alerts those in the saloon of the posse' return.

I take it as my cue to go on my way. Turning on my boot

heel, the gambler catches me by the arm. "Don't you want to make sure that's not your husband, Darlin'?"

Oh, he'd love it if something happened to the bounty hunter. That's not his horse carrying the body. The bounty hunter rides a roan stallion, not a dark-haired mustang. Still, the thought of losing Chord sends an invisible arrow into my heart. Over these past couple of months, the man has woven his way into my heart. I didn't expect to feel anything for him. He didn't ask me, either. A woman doesn't get married to a man like the bounty hunter and not feel something. Each time he's kissed me I've felt a whole lot of something, and it down-right makes me want more of those kisses and ties with an invisible lasso drawing me closer to him.

It's the last thing he wants.

I'm not his wife. Not really. Not in the Biblical sense, anyway.

I bristle a bit, taking a step back as my heart rises in my throat choking out any words to come.

Deputy Payne comes through the crowd, making his way from the saloon. I tip my hat down and step behind the gambler. He quirks an eyebrow at me.

Down at the sheriff's office, one of the local ranchers steps forward. "We chased them outside of Silver Valley."

"You got one of them?" Payne looks a bit peaked.

If I didn't skedaddle along, I'd lose the light to aid in putting distance between me and the deputy. Surely, the bounty hunter hadn't meant for him to keep me locked up the entire time he was gone. Plus, the bounty hunter had a good day's lead on me.

"No," another cowboy says, holding his hat between his hands in front of him. "One of us is dead, and we left two more injured in Silver Valley with the doctor."

The first man to speak added, "Figured it would be best to

get back and report to the sheriff. Many of us have ranches to tend and couldn't keep going on the chase."

"If you didn't get one of the outlaws, who is this?" Deputy Payne asks, sounding a little relieved.

"Buck Dawson." The second cowpoke lowers his head.

Murmurs go through the crowd until, out from nowhere, a scream burst in the whispers. I know that shrill. Amaryllis shoves and pushes past those in her way to get to Buck's mustang. The gambler and the cowpoke rush to keep her from grabbing the wrapped body. The gambler spins her around while the other man grabs the reins of the horse and gets the body out of there.

She sobs and screams as they try dragging her back toward the saloon.

As the deputy invites the ranchers inside, I take my cue to slip away and make a run for my horse.

6

Halfway toward the mountains, I bring my faithful pony, Lulu, to a halt. My heart pounds as fast as my mind races. The posse came from Silver Valley. Which didn't mean the gang hadn't split and went in two separate directions. The bounty hunter mentioned heading for the mountains. One way or another, the bad guys won't get away.

They could have each taken their share of the money.

How am I going to get it all back?

My heart aches for all the folk who lost their hard-earned cash. And Buck. The Dawson family has lost their eldest son. Now, my friend Ella Mae's husband, Lincoln, will inherit the ranch, but no one should lose a family member like this. Which gang member had killed him? They would have more of a bounty on their head. Robbery. Murder.

Lulu tugs at my reins. The mountains are calling, but would I run into the bounty hunter on my way? Would he try to stop me again?

Silver Valley, here I come.

Lord, you have a mean way of keeping a girl from getting what she wants. Deciding I'd better listen, I head toward Silver Valley. It's a day's ride opposite of my beloved mountain home. If God wants to go through all the trouble to keep me out of the mountains, I figure I should obey.

Ella Mae will get a good laugh when I tell her all this. Oh dear, Ella Mae. How must she feel about all this? As my best friend, I'm torn between going out to see her or riding through the night to reach Silver Valley.

Buck's dead. I can't save him, but what I can do is find his killer and get the town's money back. Ella Mae will understand. She's one of the most righteous people I know.

While my heart sinks, having to turn my back on my claim and those on the mountain. If I know the bounty hunter at all, I know if there are bandits hiding amongst the claims, he'll find them. I pray Tail Feathers don't find him first. They don't always take to strangers and while the chief and his warriors met my new founded husband; it doesn't guarantee his safety. I agreed to allow the railroad to tunnel through my piece of the mountain to keep them protected. I should have made sure Chitto, more than Tail Feathers, understood no harm could come to the bounty hunter or our deal would end.

But first, I need to catch the robbers. The bounty hunter has been doing this long before I came into his life. I've got nothing to worry about. Or do I?

Clucking and giving Lulu a nudge in the direction of Silver Valley, I give the mountain one last backward glance.

Sure, the bounty hunter might get upset with me. But I need to do this. I need to prove I can do this.

Which was why I have to go to Silver Valley. Sooner or later, the bounty hunter will catch the outlaws who ran for the hills and come looking for the others. I plan to have them turned into the local law way before he arrives. After all, we are partners for life. He might not want me going with him to ensure I stay safe. Of course, I know the real reason is he fears I'll slow him down.

A girl doesn't grow up on the mountain not knowing how to survive.

I add a whispered prayer for the bounty hunter, and another. The guilt gets to me, so I add one for Amaryllis. For all the woman's fault's I saw the way she cared for Buck. Probably more than she did my father, or so she claimed back when I suspected her of murder. It wasn't my place to judge the woman's decisions. As I saw it, she made her choice, having gone to the ranch with Buck, then returned to the saloon. A place I refused to step foot inside again after my father lost both me and our claim by gambling. Thanks to the bounty hunter, I have my land back. And in the process, Chord and I ended up hitched. Despite what some judge says or how the bounty hunter or even the gambler feels, I don't need a man.

What I need is to find the trail where the posse left off.

Time runs against me as the sun sinks lower and lower on the horizon. It's beautiful, the way the blue-gray turns to a darker navy, and the sun glares, smearing it with the orange and reds like a campfire. Pink edges pull into the night and soon I won't be able to see much further ahead of me. Lulu can see better, but traveling through the night isn't fair to my paint pony. I need her roaring to go in the morning. Somebody has to catch those robbers before they can spend the town's hard-earned money.

Directing Lulu off the main trail into Silver Valley, we take what appears to be a deer path between the trees, leaving the open plains behind. No longer can I look back and see any signs of Deadwood. If I ride through the night, I can make it to Silver Valley by morning, but the chance of running into more thieves or murders is too great to go riding in blind.

Once we're down off the road far enough, I halt Lulu. There's a gigantic oak, and some bushes clustered together. Sliding off,

Lulu gives a soft snort. Giving her a pat on the neck, I find a few handfuls of oats in my saddlebag for reward. There's no creek near, so my paint pony will have to wait for water. My entire canteen will seem like nothing more than a sip to an animal this large.

After tossing my saddle down, I find a bite of jerky. Soon I'm saying a prayer for the Lord to bless Ruby and her thoughtfulness. She even wrapped some cold-cooked bacon in there. My chest tightens thinking of how much she's been like a mother to me all these years.

It doesn't take long to get a small fire blazing. I keep my saddle and my body leaning back against the big oak. It blocks anyone from peering down off the road and finding me in the morning. Not that it will matter if they catch sight of Lulu's big arse sticking out of the bushes.

When the sun slips away and Lulu and I are left in darkness, every sound scrapes at my ears. It's too cold not to build a fire, but it feels too far away as I prefer to keep leaning against the tree. The flames could put a girl in a daze if she's not careful. The bushes rattle and the wood crackles from the fire. Shorty sits across my lap, ever faithful, like my steed. All the times I've ever been alone were on the mountain in the shack my father built. Out here in the open, in the dark, with no walls, a shiver ripples through me. My coat is warm, and thoughts of the bounty hunter who bought the coat for me, adds to the warmth. Maybe moving to the fire for a while won't be so bad.

I have never been a fan of dark and small enclosed places. While I'm not in a small place, I swallow down the apprehension and question why on earth I didn't wait it out until morning at Ruby's. I could have hidden somewhere from the deputy. That way, I'd ride all day and arrive in Silver Valley by nightfall.

Taking a deep breath, I hear a twig snap. Lulu's shadow

stays by the bushes. But the eerie stretch of darkness has me gripping Shorty by the barrel. I take my hat and let it fall to hang off my shoulder. The hat string tickles my neck and as I reach back to scratch, a hand grabs mine while another clamps over my mouth. I scream, but the hand muffles it. Striking out, the figure straddles me and pins me against the tree. His deep voice stuns me, and my mind works to catch up with his foreign words.

My heart skips a beat and slowly, the hand over my mouth comes off. "Why are you alone?"

Chitto, my childhood friend, and the man who gave me Lulu, crouches over me. He keeps my wrist as his captive.

"Why are you scaring me half to death?" I say back at him, and then lower my voice. "What are you doing here?"

"I knew, sooner or later, Man Killer would leave you alone," Chitto says. "You should have stayed in the mountains. You are safer with me."

I pull Shorty closer with my free hand. My heart pounds as it tries to calm after the scare. Pushing Chitto, he releases me and sits back by the tree. "You're not safe. I'm the one trying to keep you safe."

In the firelight, his white tooth grin lights up in the dark. "You say you marry the one who kills men for a living because he protects you, but yet you look after the ones you care about. Willow, woman of Stands With Two Deer, is a furious warrior."

Stands With Two Deer is Chitto's adult name. When warriors become men, they are given a new name, but he'll always be Chitto to me. "I'm not your woman. I'm married to the bounty hunter."

Chitto snorts softly, and his grin goes away. "Where is your bounty hunter? These laws of the people beyond the mountain are they written in blood? Them and their paper, they burn and tear. It does not last."

If I didn't know better, I'd think he and the gambler had met. Ever since the gambler caught wind that my marriage may be in name only, he's been trying to prove it, so the judge will give me an annulment.

"Who told you such a thing?"

Chitto tosses another stick on the fire. "I scout for the railroad now. Men talk."

Crossing my arms, I keep Shorty close to my body. "What are you doing here? Shouldn't you be looking for a route for the train tracks to go?"

Chitto shakes his head. He's got dark eyes and a hawk-like nose. His long black hair hangs down his back. It would be a lie to say I am not happy to see him.

"No place for tracks. They dig. It will take them until the snow falls. The railroad man, Connor, he wants to return to town. I take him. I see you leave. I follow."

Connor? "You mean Conway?"

"He give me this." Chitto pulls out a piece of paper from his waist pouch. "It give me permission to roam so I can scout and no man give me trouble."

"Most men shoot first and ask questions later," I say.

"I have one of those." Chitto rises to his feet. Soundlessly, he disappears into the darkness. A few moments later, he returns, a rifle in one hand, and a blanket in another.

"Where did you get that?" I hiss, hoping he didn't steal it.

"Man Killer," Chitto lays his blanket not far from mine. He holds the rifle in the light to inspect it. "Good gift, but Willow, still my wife."

Willow is my middle name. It's the name Chitto has always called me, and Man Killer is the name Tail Feathers's tribe gave the bounty hunter. Our time on the mountain didn't serve to gain their support. While there, we brought them gifts and made a deal with Tail Feathers to keep them safe and allow the railroad to come through the mountain without their inter-ference.

Even in the dark, with the shadows dancing between us, the look Chitto gives me could terrify the devil. I've seen him look at enemies much the same way, and I've seen him look at me in broad daylight. Once, long ago, it would have made my knees knock and my toes curl.

He's got nothing on the bounty hunter. While Chitto may have been a young girl's fancy, the bounty hunter fills a woman's head with hopes and dreams of a future.

We spend the rest of the night with Chitto keeping watch, Lulu by the bush, and me trying to figure out my next move once I get to Silver Valley. One thing is for certain. I can't let Chitto tag along. There's not a territory in Utah that would welcome him. I've got too much to worry about besides keeping him alive.

When I feel him try to lie next to me, I remind him I am another man's wife. I may still have one pony Chitto gave my father as a bride price, but the bounty hunter and I stood before a judge and, by law, Chord Townes is my husband. Twice now I've been a bride, and twice I haven't found out what it is like to become a true wife. I guess I'll have to make the third time count.

The bounty hunter says he'll let me go when the right man comes along. In name only or not, I already have a husband. Now, to convince him I'm worth keeping, but I know he's got a broken heart and time can torture one's soul.

7

By morning, I'm ready to leave the hard ground behind. I didn't realize how soft a girl could get living in town and sleeping in a big comfy bed every night.

Stretching to get the kinks out of my back and wake up my arm and hip, I yearn for a cup of black coffee. With those thieving killers ahead of me, coffee will have to wait until I get to town. Ever since the bounty hunter introduced me to a little cream in my coffee, I've been addicted like a brave to a smoking pipe.

Chitto comes out of the bushes, and I take my turn. He's got this look in his eyes and it makes me sigh.

"You can't go into town with me."

Chitto crosses his arms, stands in my way of getting Lulu saddled, and gives me that same look of a man who won't take no for an answer.

"You have gone to the place before?" he asks.

"No." How different can Silver Valley be compared to Deadwood?

"This is not good place for woman to go alone."

"How do you know?"

"Why do you think Man Killer would keep you tied like pony?"

I shouldn't have told him the part where the bounty hunter cuffed me, and the deputy tried to keep me in town. My lips get loose when I'm tired and it's dark, and the sound of a voice can keep the fear from raising. Not that I'm afraid of being alone. I have no love for the dark, is all.

"It's my money. The whole town lost their hard-earned savings. I can't let them get away with it." I huff. The saddle gets heavy in my arms. Fresh brewed coffee awaits me in town. The phantom scent of it tries my patience.

Chitto continues to stare at me. A brave can spend hours watching and waiting for the right moment to strike their prey. Maybe one day I'll introduce him to good coffee. He'll understand my haste, but for now, I say, "The bounty hunter went in the opposite direction. He doesn't know Buck Dawson is dead, and I'm not letting them get away with it."

Chitto's lips press thin. Behind those dark eyes, he contemplates my words. I say them again, this time in the language of his people. "You find Man Killer. Tell him what I have told you."

My arms burn with effort to hold the saddle.

"And you will not try to capture these men before Man Killer finds you?"

Chitto knows me too well. He once saved me from a mine collapse when I was younger. A cold drip of dread trickles down my spine. My father hadn't even come looking for me when I'd been gone for several days.

Even now, I won't admit having Chitto on the other side of the tree let me sleep with both eyes closed.

"I won't." I say, "But I need to find them."

My intuition tells me to follow the road to where the fire-water flows freely, and the cards are dealt with a sleight of hand. Lord, help the men who stole my money and killed Buck Dawson. Because I'm coming after him.

"I promise," I add quickly, seeing Chitto's expression harden.

"Your promises are false." He takes the saddle from my arms.

A thousand squiggly worms race across my flesh at the relief of the burden taken from them. I suppose I have it coming to me. Although, I never promised to marry Chitto. He tied his ponies outside my father's shack, and I fed them. When my father saw the ponies, he decided he needed me to fix the biscuits and brew the coffee, so he kept us both, the ponies and me. Chitto always said he could wait—until the day his cousin's wife matched him with another. I've long gotten over the infatuation of the brave's kisses. Some men have a hard time moving on and are especially forgiving.

There's no forgiveness in Chitto's eyes.

There is no hurt in my heart for the woman he made his wife.

Only a deep yearning to know what it is she knows about her husband that I haven't found out about mine.

By the way, Chitto keeps reminding me about the ponies. I doubt he'll get over it soon. He took the name Stand With Two Deer because he claims he has two wives. It doesn't matter how many times I explain to him about one man and one woman.

One of these days I'll have to give him Lulu back. Even then, I'm not sure he'll get the message. He knows the bounty hunter and I are hitched. We shared a lodge in Tail Feather's camp—a lodge, not blankets.

The bounty hunter isn't much for cuddling.

With the sun peeking through the trees, the morning will soon slip away. It's time to get moving and get back on track.

"What would you have me do?" I challenge Chitto. "You know me better than to let a fox steal from the henhouse. What they took would have secured me for a long time. And other folks too. You can't tell me you and a bunch of other braves from your tribe wouldn't have chased after them. They killed a rancher, and they can't get away with it."

Lulu snorts in agreement.

Chitto, with his wool clad back to me, finishes cinching the girth around Lulu. Braves don't saddle their ponies, and it makes me wonder how many other things he knows about the world beyond the mountain. "Our laws are not the same. I will see you to this place or you will not go."

For the first time since we awoke, and the sun lifts the foggy haze, I notice Chitto's wearing a cavalry issued jacket and pants, much like the ones Brody Brownell and his gang wore.

"Where did you get that?" I point to his clothes.

Glancing down at himself, I follow his gaze to the brown laced up fur boots going down from his knees. "I blend."

"Please say you traded for those."

A wicked grin spreads across his face. "He no longer needs them."

"Are you crazy?" I hiss. "You can't go killing soldiers. That's bad. Very. Very. Bad." I pace in circles. My hands digging into my hair. My hat swinging against my back from the cord around my neck. Like a hangman's noose, it pulls taunt and I struggle to breathe. "I told you. Killing is bad."

Two firm hands land on my shoulders. "I no kill. Man already dead." He shows me the hole in the jacket down close to the waist. There is a slight stain. "I blend," he says again. "I go with you. I not let my woman ride amongst strangers alone."

Ignoring the last part, I ask, "If you didn't kill him, who did?"

Chitto shrugs.

"At least tell me where you found him. He was dead, right?"

He points in the direction east.

"Dead?"

"His soul walks without him."

This can't be good. I glare at Chitto. The last thing we need is the Cavalry hunting him down over a dead soldier. Or was it a soldier? It could have been Brody or one of his gang.

"What did he look like?"

"Dead man," says Chitto.

Trying to hold in a groan of frustration, I grab Lulu's reins. "Show me."

Chitto's pony stands several yards away. He's a black beauty with feathers braided in his mane.

Once I am settled on Lulu's back, Chitto grabs his horse by the withers and gracefully glides on bareback. One thing is for certain, if Chitto plans on riding into town, he'll need a saddle. Something tells me that's an even worse idea and another dead body on the trail to Silver Valley.

It doesn't take us long to reach the place where Chitto found the dead man. He's not far off the road. His body stripped down to his long underwear and a trail of blood from the road to where he rolled down over the hill.

"He must have fallen off his horse,"

"Did you see one?"

"No horse." Chitto nods toward town. "Tracks are many. Whoever did this, they took horse."

I nudge the body with my boot. "Why would they kill him and steal his horse?"

"Whoever kill man not want the spirit to ride into the great plains of the afterlife of your people," Chitto says.

"We call that heaven." At least those of us who believe in God. Chitto and his people have a different version of who God is and believe in the one called the Great Spirit. I make a note to see about bringing a Bible or two into Tail Feathers's camp. The few who can read English may try to read it to the others. I wonder if that would make me sort of a missionary, like the ones Ella Mae spoke of once going out to spread The Word to desolate miners.

Then again, I can't be a missionary and chase down robbers at the same time. Inspecting the body, I cover my mouth, feeling sick. "Gut shot."

"Is he one of your outlaws?" Chitto asks.

Shaking my head, there isn't much to left on the body. His boots are missing, but Chitto's wearing his own boots. Even in death, the man appears in pain, and his eyes are vacant as an empty kettle by the fire.

"You want to bury him?" Chitto doesn't sound at all interested in the task.

"No. I'm taking him to town."

Chitto frowns. "You recognize him? How much he worth?"

"I don't know." I flip my braid off my shoulder and stand straighter. "But either way, he could be valuable."

Chitto reaches for the knife in his belt and bends towards the body.

"What are you doing?" Panic flares inside me.

"Scalp. Worth money."

My stomach flips, and not in a good way. "No! You can't scalp a man."

Chitto shrugs and straightens. "What else dead man good for?"

"You didn't kill him?" I ask again, trying to get my beating heart to slow down. Lulu swishes her tail and for a minute I swear I can feel a drop of heaven's tears on my nose.

"You do not believe the word of Stands With Two Deer?" His chest puffs out.

"I believe you took his clothes. Now, help me. We need to get this bad guy to town." If he's a bad guy at all. But something tells me whoever this man is, he's going to help me find the robbers.

Taking a deep breath, I rub my hands down my riding skirt. The man couldn't have been much older than me. Grabbing him under the shoulders, I try to lift him. He's as stiff as a board. I groan with the effort. "Well, don't stand there. Help me," I say.

"Dead man, no walk," Chitto says.

"Grab a blanket and we'll roll him into it and toss him over your horse."

Chitto unties the bedroll from my saddle.

"Not my blanket!" I drop the body. Jump back as guilt washes over me right before I'm relieved as I remember the man's dead and can't feel anything.

"Then what blanket do you speak of?"

I blew a curly piece of hair from out of my view. He may have the man's clothes, but braves don't carry bedrolls behind their saddles. Chitto doesn't have a saddle on his black beauty.

"Fine," We'll just tie him around you and it'll look like he's riding double."

Chitto snorts. "Willow woman has crazy ideas. No wonder Man Killer tries to keep her locked up."

"How else do you suppose we get him to the sheriff in Silver Valley?"

A grin splits open on Chitto's face. "This mean Chitto go with Willow into town."

Opening my mouth to object, quickly I close it. Scowling at him, his grin widens into a full tooth smile.

"Fine. We'll tie him to me, and I'll take him in." I groan inwardly as a thousand invisible spiders crawl over my flesh. "This better be worth it," I mutter more to myself than the brave striding closer to me.

We each grab a shoulder and try to push the body to its feet. The body slides forward, so I move to the front and step on the feet. Forcefully, Chitto pushes the body, and it goes straight up and slams into me. I'm a big girl. The stench coming from under the body could drop a grizzly instantly.

Turning my face away and holding my breath, I try to swivel the body around and walk it toward Lulu.

My pony side steps away as the body gets closer. Her eyes bug out the side of her head and I talk gentle-like to her. Never known a horse to spook at a dead person. Then again, I haven't ever been this up close and personal with one like this before, either.

Not even when my father died, and I went to view his body. I'd gone to find the photo and the deed I hoped he had in his boot. They were missing, as was one of his boots. At least someone hadn't stolen both. Who would kill a man, take his horse, and leave his boots?

Bank robbing, horse thieving, outlaws, that who!

"You sure we do this?" Chitto asks.

I can tell by the way he's holding the body away from him, he's rethinking this as much as I am.

"Of course. Now hold him while I get Lulu."

"You will have to get on first, but I can't lift this body alone." Chitto has the tone muscles of a seasoned warrior. He's filled out nicely since we were adolescents. And, yes, I'm still a married woman. A girl can't help noticing things.

"Well, tie his arms around me and when I get up, you can help get him behind me."

Hopefully, this works. I say a brief prayer as Chitto comes in front of me. The body leans heavily against me. Chills creep over my face as the body's flesh comes into contact with my cheek. I bite my lip from making a disgusting sound.

The arms are stiff. Chitto wraps a leather cord around the wrist, tying them together below the sisters. Ain't no one getting their hands on my most precious assets. With my money gone, all I've got left to lure a man with is my curves, and any man who tries to get a hold of them will need a signed license by a judge. I happen to know one man in particular who has just that.

Lulu jerks away and Chitto commands my pony in his language to stand. She's not having any of this, and dances around. Hoping around on one foot, I try for the saddle horn, the stirrup, anything. The body tied to me falls back and Lulu slips from my grasp. I go flying back and land on the stiff behind me.

There's no getting up from this. Twisting and getting to my side, I try to launch up, but the body is dead weight holding me down. Those cold, pale hands are below the sisters, making it hard to breathe. Digging my boot heels in for traction, this body isn't going anywhere.

I hear Chitto talking to Lulu.

"Help me!"

"I am here," he says, then the next I know he's grabbing the hands below the sisters and up we come.

Lulu is tied to a tree with black beauty not far away. Chitto unties the hands that bind me to the outlaw's corpse. Together, we toss the body over Lulu's saddle and tie it down.

Next thing I know, I've got a leg up on Chitto's black beauty and he jumps up behind me. His arm rest under the sisters, much warmer in place than the dead outlaw. I shiver with the thought, and Chitto murmurs in my ear. "Do not worry, Willow. Death cannot reach you in my arms."

Maybe not, but twice in two days it's come within my path. If this is any sign of what is coming, then I should hit the jackpot in Silver Valley. Them robbers won't stand a chance.

8

Riding into Silver Valley, a dead man on a horse and Chitto at my back, is bound to draw a few glances in our direction. We arrive in town around noon. My stomach grumbles in protest of having missed a good drowning in coffee. The dried venison Chitto shared with me an hour back has worn off.

Standing outside the jail, it's as if the sheriff got wind we were coming. He leans against the porch post, his hat tipped up. Silver Valley's sheriff isn't at all what I'd imagined. He's got hair as white as the fallen snow on the mountain peaks and a set of six shooters rests on both thighs. His hands aren't the least shaky, and he steps out of the shade to greet us.

"What do we have here? A dead man, a woman, and an Indian." While his tone doesn't seem the least insulting, it gets under my skin. He rests those hands on the butts of his guns. Seeing him do that makes me miss the bounty hunter. I sigh as Chitto reigns his horse closer. "You sure this is good idea?"

No, but it's the only plan I've got.

"Afternoon. Sheriff, is it?" I bat my lashes like Miss Daphne Davenport taught me. Maybe all those lady-like lessons she tried to import upon me will be of good use after all. One would think after I tried to save her life, she would be more grateful to me. Maybe during our descent down the hotel stairs, more than her ankle got twisted. Maybe like poor Sherman, the desk clerk, her head got a little rattled, too. Either way, Miss Davenport no longer considers herself a friend of mine. Not that I'd consider us friends, not the way Ella Mae and I have been so close.

Another reason, I have got to catch these robbers and get back to Deadwood. My heart aches for the Dawson family.

"Silvester McCullough. Most folk around here call me Sheriff Silver. Now tell me what a curly haired woman is doing riding in with an Indian and a dead man on a horse?"

He narrows his eyes on Chitto. Carefully, I untie the body and slide down from the horse first, then Chitto follows. We drape the dead man across Lulu's back to keep it from hitting the dirt.

Chitto keeps his chest pressed to my back and the reins of both horses gripped in his hands.

"I came to check for the bounty on this man. I believe he's one of the outlaws in the Brownell gang."

The sheriff takes a walk around Lulu and takes a good long look at the body. He shakes his head and comes back to me. Looking between Chitto and myself, I get the feeling the sheriff is trying to decide which one of us he should address. While it's common for men to address each other before a woman, Chitto's not high on the admittance list for the kind of folk welcomed in town.

"Well?" I ask, taking the decision out of his hands. I cross my arms. "Is there a bounty on this man or not?"

The sheriff has a wicked gleam in his eye, and it's directed more at Chitto than me. "Do you always kill men and try to find out if they're wanted later? What happened to his clothes?"

Chitto presses forward. I put my hand up to hold him back.

Sheriff Silver raises his brow.

"He was that way when we found him."

I can see the doubt in the sheriff's face, but he's not going to pin this on Chitto. Inside, my every nerve is screaming to tell Chitto to get on his horse and run like an avalanche is after him. He should have listened to me as we got closer and left me walk the horse and the body in town.

Chitto can be the most stubborn brave I've ever met, that or he's plain stupid and I'm too nice to admit it for both of us.

"You want me to believe you found a dead body and brought it to town with you on the chance it might make you some money?"

"If we killed the man, do you think we would bring him to you otherwise? He either has a bounty on his head or he doesn't?"

The sheriff scratches his chin. The bowler hat on his head shifts with the movement. "Not everybody alongside the road is an outlaw. What's a woman and an Indian doing on the road?"

"Willow is…"

I give Chitto a look to keep his mouth shut and try to handle it. "I'm after the Brownell gang. They robbed the bank in Deadwood and killed a rancher. I believe this man is one of the members of their gang."

"And the Indian?" Sheriff Silver asks.

"He's a scout for the railroad. If you haven't heard, it's coming through the mountains and into Deadwood."

"Then what's he doing here with you?" Sheriff Silver asks.

I notice we're gathering the stares of a few locals standing across the street.

Chitto lands his hand down on my shoulder. "I protect."

"He works for my husband," I say.

"I thought he's a scout?" Sheriff Silver says.

"He is. He does both." I take a deep breath. "You don't

think my husband would let me out running across this wild country alone, do you?"

The sheriff reaches for my left hand. He inspects my fingers and I hear Chitto draw a deep breath. *Lord, help this man keep his cool. He's good at it any other time.*

"For a married woman, you don't have a ring. I hear the Indians don't give their women rings or marry like we do. You sure he isn't your husband?"

"Willow is…"

I cut Chitto off, give him a wicked bump in the ribs with my elbow. "Married. I'm married to the bounty hunter. You may have heard of him. Chord Townes."

Way to go Jo. I let it rush out all too fast.

"Townes? As in the Texas Ranger gone rogue?"

Who hasn't heard of my husband? And why do so many people know him? I'm beginning to think he's as famous as an outlaw. But isn't the bounty hunter the one keeping the law? Or at least bringing in the bad guys?

"That's the one," I say.

"I thought his wife was dead," the sheriff looks even more suspiciously at me.

"Yes, and then he married me. We're sort of newlyweds, so you can understand why he sent an escort with me."

"Newlyweds," the sheriff intones.

I nod like a fool. "It's been a crazy month. We haven't had a chance to pick out a ring." Saying it sours my stomach. I pull my bare fingers from the sheriff's grasp. Why hadn't I thought of it before now? Why would the bounty give me a ring? The judge hitched us with the smack of his gavel. Maybe a man only gave a girl a ring when he intended to give her more than his name. Or maybe the bounty hunter had no intention of holding on to me long enough to need one. He told me he'd let me go when another man was worthy of me. Maybe I don't need a ring because soon he'll marry me off to someone else, just not the gambler.

All this time, the sheriff has been staring at me. Finally, he gives a nod and takes a step toward the office. "Have your Indian take the body down to Woodberry for a box. It's down on the other side of the street and take a turn or two to the left."

Chitto doesn't budge.

"Go on."

"Where you are, I am," he says.

"Mrs. Townes and I have business in my office. Unless, of course, you don't want that bounty."

"I wait here, then go."

The sheriff shrugs. "Have it your way."

I follow him into his office, leaving Chitto with the horses.

"Don't worry, you can see him from the window." The sheriff tosses his hat on the desk. Inside, the office is larger than Sheriff Bentely's. There is a door to the side. I'm guessing that's where the holding cells are located.

On the wall behind him are three rifles and a bunch of posters on the wall. All of them have a big 'x' over the faces.

"So, is he one of the gang? The dead man?" I ask.

"Can't be certain. Don't see many of their faces, just the two leaders, Brody and his brother Irwin. I'd say if he is, then he's a new one added to the bunch. Last I heard, there were five of them. Now, maybe four."

He goes around his desk and pulls open the drawer. Inside, he pulls out a little lock box. "I heard about the robbery. A posse came through here yesterday. You're a day late if you think to keep on their trail. Does your husband know you're out chasing outlaws, Mrs. Townes? Or are you chasing him?"

"Why would I chase my husband?" I try not to sound as offended as I am and laugh it off.

"Why does a woman going around without a wedding ring have an Indian wearing a Calvary uniform as an escort?"

"He's a scout," I defend.

"I heard the Calvary enlisted a few of the natives. Matter of fact, word has it there is a division headed toward the mountains to protect the railroad going through."

My heart jerks to a sudden stop. Calvary. In the mountains? Did Conway do this? Did he know about this? More importantly, did the bounty hunter?

"If I were you, Mrs. Townes. I'd head back to Deadwood and wait for your husband there. Leave the chasing of outlaws to the law. If Townes married you like you say he did, I doubt the man is looking to bury another wife." He slaps ten dollars on his desk. "This should get you where you're going."

"Ten dollars?"

He takes a seat. "That body doesn't have a name. You're lucky I am going to take you on your word you found him dead. Deliver him to Woodberry or bury him outside of town on your way out."

"Who says I'm leaving?" I take the ten dollars and stuff it in my skirt pocket.

"If the Brownell gang were here, they wouldn't have stuck around long. Go home and find yourself a husband." He winks.

"They might try to rob the bank here in town."

"Brody Brownell is no fool. He might have led a posse to believing he was headed here, but he and his men are probably halfway to Rapid City by now. Don't you worry your pretty little head over catching them. Go on back to Deadwood. Take your Indian with you and if I see your bounty hunter husband, I'll send him home to you."

By the twitch of the sheriff's lips, somehow, I find it hard to believe.

Outside, Chitto stays by the horses. Several men have gathered to glare at him. A few cross the street and head in our direction. "We should go," Chitto says.

For once, the sky is a cheerful blue and not a cloud in sight. The air surrounding us, however, seems to go dry and choke a person with the insufferable attention coming our way. And the last thing we need is another storm of trouble brewing.

The sheriff doesn't bother looking out his window. I draw my shoulders back and take my horse's reins from Chitto. "That's what the sheriff said, too. Come on, I am not going anywhere until I find those thieving bandits."

Chitto glances over at the men and looks at me wearily. I take Lulu and head down the street. Several men approach, and I tilt up my chin. Shorty hangs beneath the body tied to my saddle. "What? You never seen a dead body before?" I say, leading Lulu closer to them.

"It isn't the body," one of the replies.

"Surely you men have seen a woman before. If not, you should visit the dance hall. I hear you can find a pretty one to dance with you for a dollar," I say.

Lulu nods her head in agreement as we try to shove through them.

"Got a pretty girl right here," the same man says, "But that's not what we're looking at."

"He doesn't have no business in this town," another says.

"He's here on official business with the Calvary. You don't want to mess with a government man, do you?"

"Seems he can't talk for himself. You speak English?" another laughs.

Chitto draws himself up. "You are standing in the lady's way."

The man's eyes widen.

"Maybe he is here on business," I say.

"Ain't no business for a Calvary man to ride into town alone, especially one of his kind," another spats.

My blood boils.

Chitto reaches into his pouch. Two of the men pull out their guns. "Whoa there! Whoa!" I shout and try to step in front of Chitto.

Slowly, my brave friend pulls out a badge on cloth given to him by the railroad to show the men.

"What's going on here?" Sheriff Silver comes jogging behind the horses. His white brows drawn together. "I thought I told you two to get out of town."

"You told us to take the body to Woodberry," Chitto says.

"You should arrest him," the first man says.

"Yeah sheriff. He's got a lot of nerve riding in here with a dead body and a woman," another says.

"Did he kill him?" the third asks.

"No!" I shout.

"She belongs to him," the first man says.

"I do not!" I grind my boot into the dirt.

"No boys," the sheriff says, but none of them listen.

"Yeah boys, go off and play," a man dressed in a black pants and a tan shirt steps in front of them. His hands are stained across the tips of his fingers. "Leave this to the real men in town."

It gathers a few chuckles and makes my face heat. "Kindly move aside, and we'll be on our way."

"You'd best do as she says, boys."

Another snicker, but the man doesn't move. "Isn't there some kind of law against killing?"

"No one killed anyone." I turn my hand into a fist.

"There's a dead man on a horse," another points out.

"The only dead man is going to be you if you do not let my woman pass," Chitto holds up his rifle.

"You hear that, Sheriff? He threatened me."

Oh no. "Chitto," I say in warning. "Let's go." I try to turn to go the opposite way, when the man with stained hands grabs ahold of my arm. "Tell her sheriff. She's confused. Her place is here amongst her own people."

"Unfortunately, there is no crime here gentleman," he's careful not to call them boys again.

"Unhand me," I say, low, my patience fading and giving way to a bout of panic. His fingers dig into my arm, and I fear the stain will seep into the fabric of my shirt.

"Let my woman go."

"I'm not your woman," I hiss at Chitto.

"I knew Townes wouldn't remarry," the sheriff says.

"But I am his wife!"

"You hear that? She's married to the Indian."

"No!" I yank my arm away and my fist goes flying before I can stop myself. My knuckles connect with a chest and his eyes grow large. "Did you just hit me, woman?"

"Do not touch her again." Chitto's expression hardens. So much for keeping our heads low and not drawing attention. The last thing we need is for the Brownell gang to know we're here looking for them.

"I'll touch her all I like," the man challenges. "I don't see no ring. That means she's up for grabs."

This time, I don't punch him. I do what Ruby told me any woman should do when they're in dire trouble. The man almost doubles over when I use my knee.

The sheriff pulls out his gun and glares at me. "That's enough. Get out of here and take the scout with you!"

But the man with the stained hands recovers quickly. He grabs for me. Lulu rears and her reins slip from my hands. She backs away and takes off to the opposite side of the street. Chitto's horse remains calm at his side.

"Oh, I'm gonna tan your hide real good for that," he says, but before he can reach for me, Chitto plows him down and a fight ensues.

I'm pushed aside as a circle of men gather around. The

man with stained hands uses his rifle to block a blow, and it's ripped from his hands. Before I can grab it, the sheriff has it. As Chitto and the man circle each other, the sheriff shoots into the sky.

Everyone stops. The stained hand man wipes blood from his lip. Quickly, Sheriff Silver aims the gun at the men. "You," he motions to Chitto. "You're going to jail."

"What about him?" I huff. "He started it."

Sheriff Silver shakes his head. "I knew the moment you both rode in, you were trouble. Let's go," he motions again with the rifle.

Chitto scowls, spits at the ground, but does as the sheriff says. I gather the black horse's reins and follow. Lulu, the ever-loyal pony, trots behind, staying close to the black and dangling the body over her back.

As the man with stained hands takes a step towards me, I hold up my fists. "Don't even think about it," I say.

"Mrs. Townes," the sheriff yells.

The man with the stained hands backs off. He licks the blood from his lip and keeps his eyes locked on mine. "Mrs? You stop by the tannery. We have unfinished business."

Not by far. I turn and take off after the sheriff and Chitto.

9

We haven't been in town for more than a day and I should have known better. The sheriff has Chitto behind bars for 'disturbing the peace', and no date of when he'll let him out.

Some of those men are trying to say Chitto kidnapped me and killed my husband. Good grief! Do these people have nothing better to do than gossip?

I look at my bare finger and think this is partially the bounty hunter's fault. But really, it's mine. I wiggle my naked fingers as I walk to the sheriff's office.

Sheriff Silver and his deputy stand near the rifles with their voices lowered. By the look on the dark-skinned man's face, the deputy isn't happy.

"You take care of that dead body?" he asks.

"You see it on the back of my horse?" I say back.

The deputy raises his brows. I guess women in these parts aren't supposed to talk back. They haven't met my biological mother, Polly. The one thing I remember is she never had an issue speaking her mind. It was the hand that came after and swatted my tail when my father told me to mind my place. I guess he didn't want me growing up like my mother. For that, I'll forever be grateful.

Earl may not have been the best father. He tried to gamble me off in a card game, but at least I'm not frail, like Daphne Davenport or the other ladies in town. Which is why I walk right up to the sheriff and tell him I'm here to see Chitto.

"I thought you left town."

"You want me to go back and tell Mr. Conway you put his scout in the Iron Bar Hotel for standing up for a woman?"

I explain to the confused-looking deputy how Mr. Conway owns the railroad, and he hired Chitto to scout the trail because no one knows the Black Hills better than those who grew up in those mountains. Remembering the sheriff mentioning the Calvary coming, I add for good measure, "And don't you think someone's not going to come looking for him when he doesn't report back to his superiors after a while?"

Sheriff Silver has the disposition of an old grizzly. Even Sheriff Bentely is more pleasant to deal with without Ruby's cooking to sweeten him.

"Go on. Five minutes."

I slip past the door and find Chitto in the far back cell. There are two other guys, one snoozing on a cot and the other stands when I walk past him. "You come to set me free?" he asks.

Feeling sorry for him, I say a brief prayer. I don't know his crime, but only God can truly set us free. I listened enough to Ella Mae and her father's sermons to know it.

"Willow."

They say prison breaks a man, and I know what's it like behind bars. Not these bars. Back in Deadwood, I planted myself in a cell a time or two to get information and protection.

"You okay?" My brave doesn't seem any worse for wear.

"The sheriff claims he can't let me go. The men they want to hang me for the man I did not kill."

"So much for disturbing the peace," I mutter. "What about the other guy? He started it."

"He's not a threat."

I huff. "Neither are you."

"They will find a reason to kill me. Even now, they plot my end. I will not go without taking at least one of them with me."

Those aren't the words I want to hear. "No one is killing anyone. They can't kill you for who you are. You didn't kill that man and they can't prove it. The rest is a brawl on the street, which is like a day in this place tops," I tell him.

"For any other man, perhaps." Chitto wraps his hands around the bars. "You must go to Tail Feathers and tell him of what has happened. Yellow Cat will find a new husband for Blue Sparrow. She will soon bring our child into this world."

My throat thickens. The idea of Chitto becoming a father causes a deep sadness inside me. Deep down, I wonder if I will ever experience children. While I often question the type of mother I'd make, maybe it's better this way. While I may never have kids of my own. Chitto wasted no time starting a family.

Had my father not taken those ponies and denied Chitto me as a wife, would I be the one about to bring his child into the world? A tiny little voice whispers, "no." While I will always remember Chitto's kisses and our long embraces by the creek, it's the bounty hunter who makes me crave things I shouldn't.

Not even the gambler could seduce me into getting my marriage annulled.

"I'm not going anywhere until I get you out of here and catch those murdering thieves," I tell him.

"You will tie my horse out back in two nights. The other one, he says people will come for him. When they break him out, I will be free again."

I shake my head. "You'll be dead. If someone comes to

break out anyone, there will be shooting and who knows if they will not kill you before they let you escape."

It's not what he wanted to hear, but I won't lie to him. This whole situation has me feeling as if I'm tumbling down the mountain side with nothing to grab to catch myself.

"You will go to Tail Feathers."

"I will send a message to Conway. I told the sheriff as much. They won't touch you as long as they think you're with the Calvary. And you have the badge from the railroad. It'll help get you out of this. Especially since I got you into it."

His hand covers mine. "You did nothing, Willow. I make my choice. I follow and I protect you."

"When you should have been back in the mountains with your family and protecting them."

Everything I have done these past few months has been to protect Chitto and his people. They are like my family. I don't need to marry him or share the same blood to have a strong attachment to the tribe who neighbors our claim and watched over me as a child. It's my turn to return the favor.

"You are also my family. I will always protect you," he says it with such conviction, and those dark eyes of his boring into my soul, I more than believe him. I love him. I always have and I always will. My hand curls over his on the bars. "Once Conway gets the message, he'll help get you out of here. The bounty hunter headed to the mountains. Maybe he's turned around already and is on his way." Maybe, and that's a big, maybe.

"I do not think they will wait for Conway. The one with stained hands, he provokes them often."

Then I'll have to do something about it. "I won't let anything happen to you," I say, meaning it.

Then I lower my voice, knowing my time is running short. "I found a place not far out of town. It's abandoned so I will take the black there," meaning his horse, "and I think I know how to flush out the robbers."

"You took the body to be buried?"

"I have a better idea." It's a long shot and most likely one of the craziest things I've ever done.

"I dislike the look on your face," he says.

I grin. "The sheriff wants me to leave town, so that's why I found the place close by. Remember what you always said about how to draw out a rattler?"

"Willow," Chitto growls in warning.

"The sheriff gave me ten dollars. It'll cost a few dollars of it to bury the man, but perhaps he can be more valuable to me after all."

"What are you up to, little fox?"

"It means I need to find some pants for the body. I'd ask you to give them back, but I think they're part of why you're still alive."

"I do not think this is wise," Chitto says in his own language.

"I didn't think you would, which is why I'm not asking you to help me. Don't worry, I'll get you out of here and I'll still flush out those robbers."

"You will go to the mountains and see Tail Feathers, then you will find Conway or Man Killer."

The snoozing man turns on his side in the next cell. I switch to speaking in Chitto's people's native language. "By then it will be too late."

Those robbers might have thought they were clever and maybe it's like the sheriff said and they tricked the posse, but I don't think so.

They'll be headed to hit another back, or home. Wherever home may be for a bunch of outlaws, I don't know. Where do the Brownell brothers come from?

Wherever they are, Jo Willow Dean always gets her man.

Not to forget Townes. Oh yes, Townes. Ring or no ring, I'm married to the best bounty hunter in the entire South Dakota territory.

"What do you plan to do?" he asks.

"Mrs. Townes," the sheriff's deputy says. "It's time to go."

This cowgirl isn't going anywhere. I smile and thank him kindly. Another lesson from one Daphne Davenport. Then I turn to Chitto and say, "The outlaw's body is going to lead us to the robbers and I'm gonna get back the money, you'll see. Sit tight. I'm going to get you out of here, *alive*, I promise."

A girl is only as good as her promises.

And there isn't enough money in the world to replace Chitto.

There are too many dead bodies being left behind, and I intend to find the men responsible before anyone else pushes up daises.

After going to the telegram office and sending a message to Ruby, I write a letter to Mr. Conway in hopes he'll return to town soon or one of his workers getting supplies will deliver it to him.

It might take a while for him to get the message.

I don't know if Chitto has this much time.

Just enough, I silently plea with God, *give me just enough time.*

When this is over, I'll go back to Deadwood and stay there for good. I'll stay with Ruby and help her run her boarding house. Maybe from time to time, the bounty hunter will come by and court me.

It's a nice thought, but men like the bounty hunter don't court girls like me. I'm not frilly or pretty. I don't spend hours quilting, cleaning, or swapping recipes with the other women.

Most of them probably don't even know how to set a snare for a rabbit. I do.

Lulu and the black are tied behind an old cabin outside of town. It's deep in the woods and I wouldn't have led my horses deep into the wilderness to hide out. By the looks of the place, it's been forgotten. The forest has climbed through the windows and the old chimney stones are tumbled to the ground. The door leans against the side, unattached, and it doesn't surprise me to find the glowing eyes of critters looking out at me.

Unless the weather turns for the worse, I think I'll let the horses have it and sleep outside. One thing for certain, it must have been here before the town. I couldn't have gotten more blessed with the discovery. Hopefully, no one else will know it's here either. I drop the body from the saddle and the outlaw stares at me. Dragging him over near the doorway of the shack, I prop him up. Geez, this guy is heavy. My arms burn and sweat pops out on my forehead. Twice I stumble over myself as I go forward, and the dead weight holds in place. Leaning him against the shack, I take a breathier. His head flops down.

If someone comes, I need them to think he's guarding the place. I don't even want to think about how long before a dead body will cause an odor for miles.

Mother nature seems to have my back on this. Summer has come in with a chill. Still, I figure I've got a few days tops, then he'll start attracting wild animals and spoil the plans I have.

One thing is for certain, he's going to need clothes. Now that I look at him, I bite my lip and debate. Ruby packed my pants in my saddle bag with an extra shirt. Bless that woman.

They're my favorite pair of pants. My only pair of pants. I'm not sure how I feel about giving them to a dead man. Anyone who sees him sitting there in his long underwear will know something is up.

Taking the pants, I lay them over the top of his legs. It's as good of a way as any to size the fit. Rolling up the legs and starting with one foot at a time, I try not to faint at the smell of his feet. By some miracle who ever stole his boots, let him keep his socks. Holy are thou, the man has an unattractive odor. Even Lulu has been keeping to the other side of the black and away from the body.

Do horses even smell? What a silly thing to consider, of course they can. Lulu knows I've got an apple in my pocket before I give it to her.

I roll up one leg and then go to bend his leg to do the other, but this leg isn't as forgiving. I have to roll down the first leg and start the second. Straddling him, I put my big butt in his face as I work the pants up the corpse's legs. The further up I get; I have to turn around and get on my knees. Grabbing the pants by the waist band I try to wiggle it under his thighs and toward his behind. They're a tight fit.

I have to rock the body from side to side and try to pull quickly to make progress. Then I come to a halt. How am I going to lift this guy's butt to get the pants up over it?

As I crouch over him, his face mocks me. The blood has all but drained from the body, leaving his skin an even sicklier white. I've handled dead animals. Dead men shouldn't be any different, but they're bigger. As he takes pity on me, the dead man tilts to the side and falls. The pants won't go up on both sides. I shove the body again. Pulling by the waist and hiking up the guy's rear end, I tug on the pants and try to get them over his wide berth.

Behind me, I hear the rustle of movement. Glancing around, Lulu munches on a bush, but the black has his head up, ears forward. I freeze. Slowly, I look around. Shorty is in my saddle, laying just inside the cabin.

I stretch a little, not wanting to let go of the progress of the pants, but needing my shotgun.

Another rustle in between the trees has me dropping the dead man by the drawers and leaping for my shotgun.

Half crawling, half laying on the ground, I pull Shorty and flip around. There in the distance between the trees, Yellow Cat, Tail Feathers's son, and Chitto's cousin sits upon a horse with paint and feathers down the animal's neck.

Slowly, he raises a hand, and I do the same. I lower Shorty, and Yellow Cat approaches. He slides down from his horse and leads the white and grey maned horse behind him.

He remains quiet, walking past me to stand and stare at the body beside the cabin. Yellow Cat has the green eyes of his mother, which is why Tail Feathers never minded me coming around while I grew up. A mohawk runs down the middle of his head and a small bone dangles from his ear.

In the silence of his arrival, he strokes his horse's neck. "Have you killed him?"

"No."

Yellow Cat nods.

"Where is Stands With Two Deer?"

"He's in jail," and I explain what happened. "What are you doing here?"

His silence is answer enough.

"I should have known. Why didn't you come into camp?"

"I watch." He points to his eyes and out. "I go further up the trail and find the men who killed that one." He points to the corpse face planted on the ground.

"Then why ask if I killed him if you knew?" I glance down. "You took his boots!"

Yellow Cat grins. "Good fit."

"No. Not a good fit. They'll think you killed him. Where is his horse?"

"The ones he rode with took it. It carries much wealth."

"The bank robbery money." My hat sways against my

back. "Where did those men go?" I don't give him a chance to answer. "They are here, aren't they?"

Yellow Cat nods.

"Where?" I ask.

He shakes his head. "I will not bury wife of Man Killer and Stands With Two Deer. I will help you bury that one." He points to the dead body.

"No. Help me dress him. I need him to lure the robbers here and set a trap."

Yellow Cat crosses his arms. We stand at equal height. "You and Man Killer made us swear to avoid interaction with others outside of Standing Rock."

Standing Rock is the place on the mountain where Tail Feathers's tribe lives. It's outside the reservation the government created for their people.

"Fine, but this is what I need you to do."

10

If there is one thing I have learned, it's trouble, likes company. Silver Valley is known for two things: the abundance of silver mines in the area and their dance hall. It's the second most popular place the men often visit outside of the saloon.

Looking down at myself, I'll never pass for what I need to do. I swore I wouldn't set foot inside another saloon after Glen, the old saloon owner in Deadwood, tried to kill me.

It's late by the time I talk myself into entering the dance hall. Music fills the room with laughter and the sounds of feet stomping. A man with a fiddle stands by a woman playing a piano. Men gather around tables and stand at a bar. Red draperies hang at the entrance, and I cringe going between them.

Women with loose tied bodices hang off the shoulders of men, and at the far end, I spot Sheriff Silver. Perhaps I'll come back another night.

For the past few days, I've checked on Chitto while the other times, Yellow Cat and I have put our trap into place. Our bait won't last much longer, and I fear by now the robbers have gone. Each time I come into town, I watch and wander around. I visited the bank, opened an account with a couple of dollars to find Chord had a few dollars of his own stashed here.

There are many things I don't know about my new husband. Things he doesn't wish for me to know. Things about his first wife and the love of his life. Terrible things, I imagine, so terrible it would make a man leave the Texas Rangers to chase outlaws in an unfamiliar territory.

My heart squeezes. How long will it take him to figure out the Brownell gang's whereabouts?

Over thinking why I came here, I spin on my cowgirl boots and head for the door. It opens, and two men, both in Calvary jackets, step inside. Taking a few steps back, I retreat into one of the velvet curtains. At the sound of a man's voice, my knees go weak. I grab the curtains and shield it in front of me.

A woman in a black dress with dark purple lace flounces toward the men. I peek out, my wild curly hair popping out of its braid, and I try to hold it back with one hand and keep the curtain covering me with the other.

"Which one of you wants to dance with me first?" the woman asks.

There is no mistaking one man's voice. I've heard it before, in the sheriff's office, speaking with Deputy Payne. That's Brody Brownell. I peer out a little more, trying to see past the red haze of curtain and the black shield of the dance hall girl. The man beside him leans one way and I jerk back, my heart hammering, afraid he might have seen me.

They move closer and I can hear the woman complimenting them on what a big gun the one carries and the other on his muscular arms. Next, I hear a man tell Brody he has to leave his gun with him. They don't take to weapons in this establishment.

Peering around again, I watch Brody Brownell pull out his six-shooter and point it at the man.

"We don't want no trouble here," the man says, hitching his thumbs in his belt. "You'll get it back when you leave."

"Better see I do." Brody twirls the gun around and hands it to the man. The other man looks at Brody before he does the same. The woman has placed herself between them, a hand hooked on each arm. "Come on handsome, dance with me," she giggles.

A new tune starts from the fiddle, and as I turn, I find a woman with a mole painted on her cheek and a frown blocking my escape. Her dark hair has strands of ribbons tied and braided. The crow's feet beside her eyes betray her age. "What are you doing behind that curtain?"

"Oh, I'm…" for once in my life my tongue gets stuck in the top of my mouth, and I can't speak.

"You can't go in there wearing that. Didn't Ginny explain it to you when you came in? No man is going to pay to dance with you, reminding them of their mothers or wives."

I glance down at myself. Mother? Wife? "But I am a wife," I say.

She makes a face. "Come to spy on your husband, have you? Well, you can scram. Ain't no wives allowed."

Holding up my hands, I say, "No. My husband's not here. You don't understand. I just wanted to see…"

She grabs my left hand. "Oh, I see alright. You here looking for a husband?" She laughs and releases my hand. "Ain't we all."

The man who took Brody and his friend's weapon comes back and stops at the sight of me.

"We got ourselves a newbie," the woman winks at the man. "Tell Ginny I'll be back on the floor as soon as I help her find some dancing shoes."

Slowly, the man runs his eyes down over me. Reaching up and pushing my hair out of the way, the other hand goes to run down the side of my skirt. I may not have been able to bring Shorty with me, but I have a knife in my boot if this fellow gets any ideas.

"I'm Andie, what's your name?" she asks, but my eyes are on the man, and she rattles on. "For a moment when I saw you, I thought one of our old gals came back. You look like her, but with those clothes." Andi waves her hand and laughs as she takes me around the corner and leads me to a set of stairs. "Polly wouldn't be caught dead looking this respectable."

"Polly? Polly Dean?" I ask.

"You know her?"

I bit my lip, determined to draw blood before admitting she's my birth mother.

"Here." The woman leads me to a room. "You can change in here. There are plenty of dresses to choose from." She steps away from me. "Leave your hair down. Are those natural curls?"

I touch my hair. "Of course."

"Oh honey, the men are going to love you. Be sure to watch your steps, though. They'll smash your toes and then you won't be able to take them for the big money."

I don't ask. I don't want to know. The way her eyes are gleaming, I'm thinking the saloon might have been a safer option.

I'm not my mother. I repeat it over and over in my head as I swap my riding skirt and blouse for a lavender number with lace over the bodice to keep the sisters well hidden from a topside view.

I keep my cowgirl boots on and roll up my skirt and blouse. Downstairs, I have enough time to stuff my clothes under a bench as the doors open, admitting two more cowboys and a man with stained hands. As soon as he spots me, I cringe.

Those dark locks swooping over his forehead cover his eyebrows. "Where's your friend? Or should I say husband?" he sounds irritatingly amused.

I draw my shoulders back until I realize the movement pushes the sisters forward. "You know my friend is in jail. You helped put him there."

"More dances for me." he holds out his hand.

"I don't think so."

"First night on the job? Don't worry, I'm good at the Texas waltz. Your toes are safe with me." He wiggles his brows. My toes might be safe, but I don't know about anything else.

"We're not in Texas," I say.

"Then I'll have to teach you an entirely different dance. Come now. I'm not a man who takes no for an answer."

I spot Andie twirling around the room with a rowdy cowhand, and the woman in the black dress is sitting on the friend of Brody Brownell. For my plan to work, I need to get close to him.

Gulping down my doubts, I ask about the man's stained hand. Sometimes a girl has to go into the snake pit to catch the blackest of them all. They don't come more vicious than Brody.

I shiver, and my dance partner takes it as anticipation. He leads me out onto the floor and gathers me close. "Don't think I've forgotten about that tanning from a few days ago."

I try to keep up with him as he leads me around on the dance floor. Soon I'm twirling and we change partners. Round and round I go from one man to the next until I land again back in the tanner's arms. His big, calloused, and stained hands are uncomfortable. The way he looks at me is as if he'd eat me alive. If the bounty hunter looked at me in this manner, I'd get flustered. This man down right makes me sick to my stomach. I can't wait until we change partners again.

Too soon, the song ends, and another begins. I spy the man with Brody get to his feet and bring the woman in the black dress with him. Andie gives me a giant grin and picks up her dress a little higher as the fancily dressed man pulls her closer.

He's got a mustache and round wire-rimmed glasses. He makes me think of a clerk or a banker.

The piano softens, and the fiddler puts down his instrument. The ping of the keys striking the notes of a lovely song echoes in the hall.

To my dismay, the couples stick together, the men roping in the woman, and my spine stiffens as my partner tries to get me to step back. I step forward instead and land on his toes. He chuckles. "You'd best watch your step. I believe stomping on my toes is what got you in trouble in the first place."

How I would love to correct him. The last thing in need is to provoke him. Instead, I try to guide him a little in the woman's direction in the black dress. It's like trying to get a donkey to climb a rocky slope.

"I believe our dance is over." Politely I try to shed him, but he's not having any part of it.

"So soon?"

"I'm not much of a dancer," I say. "You'd be better off finding another partner."

"And miss the fun of teaching you? Oh no," he tightens his hold. "This is going to be the most fun I've had in a long time. I knew the moment I saw you there was something special about you."

"Yeah," I say loud enough over the music for him to hear me. "I'm a married woman."

"Indian customs mean nothing here. Besides, if you're married, then what are you doing in a place like this?" His grip tightens more. My fingers squeeze to the bone, but I won't give him the satisfaction of making a sound.

Andi looks over the shoulder of her fellow and mouths, "you, okay?"

I shake my head and fight back the yelp of pain harboring in my throat.

Squeezing my eyes shut, I try to breathe in through my

nose, out of my mouth. I feel him leaning, the scent of dyes and leather coming on strong.

"I know Ginny fired some of the older gals to bring in younger ones. How much she offer to give you a night?"

"That's none of your business." My eyes snap open.

"It is when I aim to take you home. We've a matter to settle." By the determined look in his eyes, escaping him won't be an easy feat.

"I'm not going home with you," I try to pull away. He stops dancing and Andi approaches.

"Hey, you." She bats at my arm playfully. "Why, who do you have here? And keeping him all to yourself," she clucks.

He puffs out his chest, but his eyes don't leave my face. "Go find someone else. I've got my girl for the night."

"Are you certain about that? I heard Ginny say the new girl's dance card was full up."

"We'll see about that." He releases me. "Don't go anywhere. I'll be back."

As he stalks off, Andi grabs me by the arm. "You best stay clear of Wes. Heard he's still sore over some woman hitting him where it hurts a few days back. Go on, find another man to dance. Ginny doesn't like us standing around solo for too long."

"What about Wes?"

"Leave him to Ginny. But in the meantime, keep dancing. Happy customers are paying customers." Andi beams as a man hollers for her. She takes off in his direction.

Seeing my chance, I head for Brody Brownell. He sits watching the dancers. I sway as lady-like as I can toward him. The crowd shifts of dancers. Men move to take seats bring girls down on their laps.

I don't make it far before a woman in a pretty calico dress and shawl plows ahead of me. She has her hair twisted in a tight bun, and her shoulders knock me back a step as she walks right up to the man beside Brody. It seems he's done with dancing and has the woman in the black dress hooked on his arm. The way she's batting her lashes at him should be illegal.

"Emory McLoughlin, you've made a fool of me for the last time." The woman in the calico dress raises her hand to slap him. Brody grabs her wrist. The shock on her face mirrors Emory's. He steps away from the woman in black, who does not shy away.

"You need to go home, Anabel," Brody says. He leans close to her. "You shouldn't be here."

"Neither should you!" she shouts at Emory, but the music mutes their conversations from those who aren't standing close by.

"Go home. Now." Emory steps alongside Brody and he releases her hand.

The woman rubs her wrist where Brody held it. "I told you not to get in with the likes of him. You'll be dead, just like Ebbi." Tears pool in Anabel's eyes.

"This isn't the place." Brody nods in my direction and the woman in black. Emory motions for us to leave, but I don't. Shock keeps me standing there in my boots.

"You promised nothing bad would happen." She pulls her hand close to her heart. "Ebbi's dead and here you are living it up!"

"I told you I'd take care of you." Emory reaches for her. "You're not my husband." She sniffles. "The man I married would never let anything happen to my brother. Family comes first," she says.

Behind Brody I notice a woman in red with black net stockings and rhinestones in her hair coming our way. Behind her, Wes follows, and a coldness spreads in my chest.

"Go home Anabel!" Brody growls. "Before I send you to the same place as your brother."

She gasps, "You wouldn't dare!"

Emory puts his arm in front of her. "That's enough. Where are the children? What did I tell you about coming around here?"

"Coming here?" she plays with the ring on her finger. "You shouldn't be here. Taking care of your family is what you should be doing. And you should have brought back Ebbi's body so we could bury him. Instead, you're dancing around with other women!"

Emory grabs her by the shoulders. I shield back behind them as the woman in red gets closer. Wes's face draws taunt with intent. In another minute, they'll know I'm not one of the girls, and I'll have to figure out how to explain why I'm here.

I lick my lips nervously.

"Woman!" Emory jerks her in the door's direction. Brody moves to go with him, and I latch myself onto him. He lifts a brow but doesn't shake me off.

Glancing back, the woman in red halts. She tilts her head as Wes smacks into her back. Brody follows my gaze. A wicked grin stretches across his face. As we step into the foyer of the dance hall, he whispers in my ear, "You might have been safer back there with him."

"I think I'll take my chances." A little thrill zings through me. Here I am, Jo Willow Dean Townes, with my hand around the arm of an outlaw. A wanted man with a price on his head, and one way or another, I plan to take him in.

11

Before we make it to the door. Emory flings it open. He shoves Anabel out. Whatever she said to him made him angry, and she yells at him. "I am not going to listen to you. You're not my husband anymore!" She pulls the ring from her finger and tosses it at him before running away.

Emory shouts, going after her, leaving me standing there with Brody. He clears his throat and my cheeks blossom with heat for staring. Before I can say another word, a man comes down the stairs. For a moment, I blink, thinking I've seen twins, but this one has more of a weathered look on his face.

"You'll have plenty of time for women later," the man says. "Get Emory and let's go."

Brody turns to me, "Seems we'll have to dance another time. I'll be dreaming of these curly locks."

The man who came down the stairs walks past him, motions with his hand, and a moment later the guard comes and returns their weapons.

Brody buckles his gun belt back around his waist and holds on to another. I assume it belongs to the one called Emory.

"It's still early," I say and try to pout.

He reaches for my face, tilts it up, and recognition comes to his eyes. "Don't I know you?"

Deciding to be straight with him, I say, "You came to the jail in Deadwood."

"You were the one the deputy locked up." Brody keeps his fingers wrapped around my chin. "We've got ourselves a troublemaker, Irwin. I say we take her with us."

"Townes will come hunting for her sooner or later."

"Good. Maybe this time he'll get the message," Brody growls.

"I ain't into killing women, Brody," Irwin settles his irons against his hips. "It's bad enough what happened in the past."

"Didn't you hear me, brother?" Brody chuckles. "She's Townes woman."

Irwin reaches up and twirls his mustache. "Even more reason to let her behind."

"She'll tell him she saw us," Brody says.

"I won't," I say. "He's miles away. In fact, he's up in the mountains. Even if I would see him, you'll be gone, won't you?"

Irwin glares at me for the longest time. Those eyes are cold, hard, and calculating.

"Go find Emory," Irwin says, not bothering to look at Brody. They are so similar in features they must be brothers, or at the very least, cousins.

"Not before we send Townes a message." Brody reaches for my curly hair. "Shame, too." He leans forward, burying his face into my hair. I hold still, unsure what to do next.

Irwin pulls him back and shoves him away. "You'd best hightail it out of here unless you want to end up like Townes wife." A gleam of gold comes from one of the man's front teeth.

"You know what happened to her?" I press my hand against my stomach to keep from getting ill.

"She's dead," Brody reaches over and tugs on my hair. "Want me to show you how?"

I lick my bottom lip, my mouth suddenly dry. "Did you shoot her like you shot the other man in your gang?"

Irwin grabs me this time, his fingers digging into arm. "What man?"

"The one on the side of the road."

"Ebbi," Brody curses.

Irwin glares at him. "You found a dead man and think he's with us?"

"No. I found a man who says he's with you. Something about you owe him for a job in Deadwood."

The two men exchange looks.

On the other side of the velvet curtain, the woman in red appears. Her red painted lips turn down. "What's going on here?"

My palms sweat as my throat closes and no words come out. I'm over my head this time. I can hardly breathe when Brody pulls me in close. "Nothing here to concern you, Ginny."

"It does when I'm told there's a new girl and I didn't hire her." Ginny pulls out a fan and flops it in front of her. "Who said you could work for me?"

"It's not what you think," I stammer.

The woman's tone sounds sharper than the knife in my boot. Her fan pauses. "Please, indulge me?"

Wes stands by the velvet curtain. I step back, positioning myself between the two outlaws. Wes crosses his arms. "I found her first. I told you Ginny, she's mine."

Holding up my hands, I tell them. "I'm married. I have a husband."

"You got a ring to prove it?" Wes challenges.

Out of the corner of my eye, I see the one Anabel tossed down. I dive for it and Irwin gets it first. Something changes in his expression. "I told you to keep this on." He grabs my finger, shoves it on. Surprisingly, it fits. A bit tight, but he squeezes my fingers tight enough to turn them white. "This little charade of yours is getting old."

"Charade?" I sputter, yanking to get my fingers out of his hold. I rub them to get the blood flowing again.

"She really your wife?" Wes asks.

Oh, but I can't tell a lie. Irwin can. He wraps his arm around my waist and pulls me up against me. At the same time, I feel his gun poking me in the side. "Little minx likes to play games."

"I told you I was married," I say, glancing at Irwin, his face harsher at this angle.

Wes turns and stomps away. Slumping for a moment in relief, I stiffen, as the woman isn't done with us. "You should go. The sheriff's asking questions. You Brownells are nothing but trouble, and don't think for one moment I believe she's your wife." Ginny gives me a good long look over. "You want to stay? It's good pay? You'd be better off than with the likes of them."

"I'm a one man kind of woman." I turn away, head for the bench where I stuffed my clothes. "I'll just change and be out of your way."

"Don't bother." Brody reaches into his pocket, puts a few coins in Ginny's hands. "Those pretty red lips better stay sealed."

She laughs, a gleeful cackle. "You come see me when you're done with these two." She tugs on her skirts and turns.

I head for the stairs and Brody yanks me back. "Where do you think you're going?"

"I am not about to walk out of here in someone else's gown." Plus, I'm hoping they'll take off because my plan went south the moment Wes and that woman Anabel interfered.

"You'll take us to Ebbi," Brody says.

"No." I say, as Irwin opens the door and I'm escorted out into the evening air. The dampness tickles my lungs. Where there is moisture, there's another rain cloud forming above us.

They walk me away from the music of the hall. My heart pounding against my chest. How will I reach for my knife? It's not like I can walk around with Shorty, my shotgun, in my hand at all times.

"No?" Irwin spits on the ground. They keep me between. "I ain't asking."

"And I'm not telling." I gulp, hoping to buy time. I sent Yellow Cat back to find Conway to help get Chitto out of jail.

"You tell me where he is or you'll be having tea with the first Mrs. Townes." Brody yanks me to a halt. His hand on his gun, but Irwin stops him. "Not here."

"What assures me if I tell you, then you'll let me go? And how do I know you don't intend to shoot me in the back?"

Brody sandwiches me between the two men. He takes a fistful of my hair. "Who says we would shoot you?" A chill wraps around my throat. Brody yanks on my hair, my scalp tingling from the pressure.

"Give me his share of the money. I'll even take you to him."

"Hear that Irwin, she'll take us to him if we give her the money." Brody says.

Irwin's chest rumbles with a laugh. The sun's long gone down and it's high past the time for me to get back to the old cabin. "Ebbi's a coward, sending a woman to collect."

"Or he's injured too bad to come for it himself."

"He would have sent her to Anabel," Irwin says.

"Emory will know how to find him. We should finish him," Brody says.

"I don't care what you do. He told me to get the money, and he'd help let my friend go. Seems the sheriff thinks he killed him."

"Killed Ebbi?" Irwin laughed. "Hope you didn't notch your gun handle Brody, you hear that? Someone else is going to hang for it."

"No!" panic sets in. "Please. Give me the money. I'll take it to Ebbi, and then when he comes into town to clear my friend's name with the sheriff, you can see for yourself."

In the dark, with the lights of a few businesses open late, the sounds of the dance hall in one direction and the saloon and diner in the other. I hold my breath. Surely, someone will come passing by.

"And the sheriff will nab us. You think we're dumb?" Brody yanks on my hair again and I suck in a breath. "We can't go around town in broad daylight."

"Take us to Ebbi."

Behind Brody, the sounds of men coming out of the dance hall makes him stiffen. Two men step off the boardwalk to go around us. Neither one pays us much mind in the dark. Another lingers behind, and Irwin tells the man to mind his business.

I can't see him. All I hear is the beat of my heart in my own ears. "Let me go!"

"You heard the lady. Let her go."

I know that voice. Brody pulls me back against him. Irwin has his iron weighing in his hand, the barrel of the gun presses against my hip.

A gun cocks from behind us. "You boys have had your fun."

"Yes, sir, Sheriff," Irwin deepens his voice, says it gruffly. "Come along dear," he tries to tug me forward.

"No. Please let me go."

I hear footsteps coming closer. "You know these men, Ma'am?"

Irwin digs the end of his gun deeper into my hip. Brody loosens his hold. "Tell him you're my wife."

"They said they're friends of my husband, but I don't know them."

"What are you doing out this late?" Sheriff Silver asks.

"I came looking for my husband. I figured he was cheating on me again down at the dance hall." I play with the ring Irwin stuck on my finger.

"We were escorting the lady. No trouble here, Sheriff," Brody tries to disguise his voice.

Afraid if I call them out for who they are, Irwin will shoot me. I keep my lips tightly pressed together.

"You men go on your way. I'll see the lady home." Sheriff Silver comes closer, and Irwin turns away, his gun in front of him. He wouldn't shoot the sheriff, would he?

"Say one peep to the sheriff and you're dead," Brody grumbles in my ear. "You tell Ebbi if he wants his money, he knows where to come find it."

Both men walk away, their back to the sheriff with darkness protecting their identities. Further up, they slip down a side street and I sigh.

Sheriff Silver comes beside me, offers his arm, and as I take it, he keeps his gun in hand. "I knew you'd cause trouble the moment you came riding into my town with an Indian and a dead body. Perhaps it is you I should be looking for a bounty on your head."

"I'll be happy to go on my way, Sheriff, as soon as you release Chitto. You know he didn't kill that man, and if you let him go, he'll head back to the mountains where he's a scout for the railroad."

I clutch my clothes, realizing all this time I've hugged them in my arms. "I know how to do my job, Mrs. Townes. I sent a telegram to Deadwood. Sheriff Payne sent a message back this evening. You're quite the escape artist."

"I don't understand."

"You will after I lock you up beside your friend. Payne's

sending one of his men to collect you. Seems I was right. You might not have a bounty on your head, but you'll have to pay for your crimes."

Confused, I ask. "What crimes? You mean *Deputy* Payne? Bentely is sheriff of Deadwood, or at least he was until he got shot during the robbery and he appointed my husband Chord Townes as acting sheriff until he's better."

"You want me to believe the most notorious bounty hunter in the territory got elected as sheriff of Deadwood?"

"No." The way he says it doesn't sound at all what the bounty hunter would do. "But if he didn't put on the sheriff's star, I would have, so he agreed until Bentley got better. He took off and left Deputy Payne in charge while he went hunting down the Brownell gang. "

"And you went on the chase after the bounty hunter with an Indian and found a dead body?" The sheriff steers me towards the jail and shakes his head. "Next, you'll tell me your husband, the sheriff, had you locked up to keep you out of trouble while he was gone?"

"He did," I say, sourly.

He lets out a bellowing belly laugh. The sheriff opens the door for me. "That I can believe."

Inside, he glances at me and sighs. "I don't enjoy locking up females, but in this case, it's for your own safety." He motions for me to follow him. "You can stay beside your friend until the sheriff or one of his men comes to fetch you."

"But…"

"Put your weapons on my desk, unless you want me to frisk you." He's serious.

I put down my clothes on his desk, hike up my skirts enough to slip my knife from my boot.

"Anything else?"

"That's it."

"No gun?"

"You see, anywhere I can hide a shotgun in this dress?" I counter.

"Well then," he points to the door leading to the cells.

The man beside Chitto is still here.

"Willow?" Chitto stands from the cot.

"Good thing you two know each other," the sheriff opens Chitto's cell door. "In you go."

"What is this?" Chitto asks.

"You can't mean to put us in there together," I protest.

"You came into town together." The sheriff gives me a nudge. "Besides, you're a married woman. How do I know you're not married to him?"

"I told you. I'm married to the bounty hunter, Sheriff Chord Townes," I snap at him.

"Then he'll be relieved to find you here, and instead of in the other cell with a man who might not care about your virtue, Mrs. Townes."

The cell door slams shut, the lock turns, and before I can utter another word, the other door closes, trapping the darkness and I scream.

But the sheriff doesn't come back, and the man in the next cell awakens. While I sit on the far end of the cot, rocking back and forth, Chitto pulls me into his arms. He tells me stories, ones he has told me many times growing up together. He tries to soothe the terror clawing me from the inside out. I cling to him, but he doesn't have the same effect as the bounty hunter. Once we were trapped in a closet and the bounty hunter knew what to say, how to calm me, his voice like a soothing balm.

I try to hold it together, counting the hours until dawn. The cells in this jail are smaller. They're closed off from the rest of the office compared to the ones in Deadwood. I've never feared them as I do in here.

Chitto continues to talk to me. The man in the next cell curses but stays away. He doesn't know the language Chitto speaks, and I allow him to distract me as we are locked away from the rest of the world.

At least here, the Brownell brothers can't touch me. But another terrifying thought flutters through my brain. What if they come across my hiding place and Ebbi's body before I get back to trigger the trap?

The fact they are here in town makes me think they won't stay long. They're here for a reason. Family, maybe? Anabel and the one named Emory were married. Clearly, he's part of the gang, the brothers, and dead Ebbi. Why else hadn't they robbed the bank by now and taken off?

They wouldn't rob a bank in their own town.

Would they?

Chitto tells a story of a brave on his first hunt while I rock to find comfort. I'm not that brave and pray I'll survive throughout the night.

I'm not sure which is scarier, a bunch of murdering outlaws, the darkness closing in around me, or the fact my plan has gone and backfired.

12

Somewhere in the darkness at the edge of my dreams, I think I hear God whispering in my ear. He doesn't make much sense. Part of that might be because I don't listen very well. Ella Mae sits in the morning with her Bible and her prayer, hoping to hear God's word to direct her for the day. She learned it from her father, the good reverend of Deadwood's church. She would be disappointed to know all those hours she sat listening, waiting, and here I am, hearing Him now. I don't devote as much time as others, and yet, I hear the whispering voice say, "keep back," and another voice. Wait another voice?

Whose God talking to in my head? Didn't I hear Him? Then I listen, half awake from the dream Chitto planted in my head of running through the forest and splashing in the creek when we were children.

A gigantic explosion goes off and I jump. My heart threatens to burst apart with the sound.

Suddenly, I'm thrown from the cot on the floor. A body covers mine with a groan. My ears ring with the explosion, but I hear men shouting, a horse whining and the crumbling of the brick of the back wall.

Trying to push up, I moan. Something trickles down the side of my face.

"Willow? Are you alright?"

I try to roll over, but the body on top of me isn't budging. "Get off!"

A moment later, the body moves off me. I roll over in time to see the man in the next climb scale the broken wall. A stream of moonlight illuminates his form, and two hands pull him from what once had been a barred window. Stumbling to my knees, then my feet, hands reach for me. "Hurry, we don't have much time."

"Time for what?" I shout, pressing my hand to my ear. It's still ringing.

"Escape. We must go." Chitto grabs my arm, but there is no way for me and the sisters to slip through the crack in the wall to get on the other side. Chitto is the first to grab the bars. The wall has given way enough for him to catch the ledge from our side and heave up. On the other side, a man shouts, "Hurry!"

But I grab him, and Chitto comes back down, feet on the rubble scattered floor. "Willow, we must go."

"No!" I shake my head. Something must have come loose inside my brain. "Are you crazy!"

He gives me a look as if I am. He grabs again for the window. "This is my only way out of here. Do you think the sheriff is going to let me go? That I will live?"

"Indian lets go!"

"You'll be a wanted man, and then they will kill you! Do you really want the bounty hunter to track you down? What about your wife?"

Pain flickers in his eyes.

The door burst open from the other side, "What's going on in here!" and a moment later another shout comes, "Jail break!"

Chitto grabs the window, slips his leg over, and reaches for me. "Come!"

"No. Stay here." I try to pull him down. "Conway will come or the bounty hunter and clear your name. You're not a killer. Don't give them a reason to kill you. That man escaping has a noose around his neck. They'll kill him and you on sight."

Chitto's eyes narrow. "Then you stay."

I can't grab him tight enough. I'm climbing up the wall to pull him back down, but a gun clicks behind me. A man is holding a rifle and pointing it at me. Chitto jumps out the window and all hopes of saving his skin go with it.

Slowly, I turn with my hands up. Sheriff Silver rushes in. "What the…"

"I at least caught this one trying to get away," the man with the rifle says.

"Too bad I wasn't trying to escape," I say. "Instead of standing here with a gun pointed at a woman, shouldn't you be going after the bad guy?" I tilt my head to the empty cell beside mine.

"What's going on Sheriff?" Another shout comes from the other side of the door. "Ford Surles has escaped."

Sheriff Silver doesn't give a second glance in my direction. "What you all standing around for? Get after him!"

The man runs to the door, then stops, his rifle pointing back toward me. "What about the woman?"

The sheriff waves his hand. "Keep guard out back of the jail. If she tries to escape. Shoot her."

I suck in a breath. Shoot me?

"I'm not a criminal!" I grab the bars and shout.

The man with the rifle snorts. "That's what they all say. Just because you're wearing a skirt doesn't make you innocent." He smirks.

I cross my arms and go towards the crumbling wall. "Don't you try to go through there. You heard the sheriff. I'll shoot."

His hands tremble slightly.

I walk over, flip up the cot and take a seat. "Shouldn't you be out back, guarding the wall?"

His eyes narrow under a wide forehead filled with creases. He's not a lawman or even a deputy. He's got on a pair of dark trousers and a rolled-up sleeve shirt. Suspenders hang from one hip as if the man got dressed in a hurry to race to the jail. The way his hair flops every which way makes me believe he too got a rude awaking.

With the door open and the moon glowing through the hole in the wall, the bars of the cell outline the boundary between us.

I should have known Chitto would bail on me. The sisters have betrayed me. I cross my arms below them. Curling upon the cot, I shiver, the draft in the wall a cold reminder.

My plans, along with my allies, have turned against me. How am I going to catch the men who killed Buck and stole the town's money?

Sounds of men fixing the back of the jail mock me. The passing days have brought grey skies and an even cooler breeze in the air. Sounds of a door opening no longer excite me. The fall of boot steps landing in front of my cell brings no reaction. A jingle of keys, the lock releases, and my pulse jumps. The door opens and I raise my head, expecting to see Sheriff Silver or his deputy with the midday meal.

Slowly, as my gaze travels up, I note those aren't the sheriff's boots. The end of the duster is familiar. I swallow hard, following the length of the coat upward. A pair of steel-colored eyes meets mine.

I've never felt more in trouble than I do at this moment. Not even as I child would I cast my eyes down and be ashamed of my actions. Nope, not me. I would look Earl straight in the eye and take my butt whopping without a sound.

There's something about the way the bounty hunter looks at me. I can't stand to see. He's been silent for a long time.

I peek a glance at him.

My rolled-up clothes are under his arms. When my gaze dares to meet his, I open my mouth, but he speaks first. "Care to explain?"

His gaze travels down my attire. For the first time since Sheriff Silver shoved me in here, I remember I swapped my riding clothes for the fancy dress at the dance hall.

"Well, you see…" I say, take a deep breath and I can't lie to this man if my life depended on it.

"I don't have all day. Get changed and you can tell me all about it on the way back to Deadwood."

"Deadwood?" I shake my head, about to protest further when a flash of something deadly enters his eyes. It's downright terrifying.

The bounty hunter tosses the bundle of clothes at me. "Get dressed."

I scoop up the clothes, catch my skirt midair and stumble to get the skirt before it hits the filthy floor.

Standing there, I swallow hard. Any minute, I suspect he'll turn around to give me privacy. Time stretches between us, the air thinner in this part of the jail.

Clutching my clothes in front of me, I wait.

"Go on Dimples. Time is wasting."

"You want me to change. Here?" In front of him?

He looks pointedly at me.

My cheeks burn. "Fine. I'll meet you outside when I'm done."

He chuckles, darkly. "I made the mistake of leaving you out of my sight once. Not going to happen again."

"You're at least gonna turn around," I ask.

"No."

"How do you expect me to change with you standing there?"

His eyes hood and he gets that sultry look which puts a flutter in my tummy.

"My *wife* is seen with two wanted men and coercing with others in a dance hall, and you want me to turn my back?"

Okay, maybe he's got a point.

He pulls back his long duster, his hand resting on the butt of his gun. My pulse speeds up. Surely, he's not angry enough to shoot me. Did I misread those hooded eyes?

If I know anything about the bounty hunter, it's he doesn't back down.

"Best hurry if you don't want Silver coming in while you're in standing in your unmentionables."

"I wouldn't be standing in my unmentionables if you'd let me out and I can change later," I huff.

The bounty hunter shakes his head. "And you wouldn't be here at all if you listened to me. I'll be having a talk with Payne when we get back."

"You mean *Sheriff* Payne," I snicker.

"I'm the sheriff, Dimples," he taps the star on his chest.

I tell him about Payne's behavior. The bounty hunter leans against the cell's door jamb. "You're stalling."

"I'm not taking off my clothes. What if someone walks in?"

"You mean like Silver?" The bounty hunter asks.

"Or his deputy," I say.

"Then you better hurry."

Huffing again, I toss down my clothes on the cot. I'm not going to win this one. If I want out, I'm going to have to strip to my knickers and dress real fast.

"Close your eyes."

He shakes his head, lowers his chin, and my gut tells me I'm done for. If dressed the part, then one should act the part, right?

Slowly, I pull down the shoulder of my dress. Tugging, it doesn't budge. The sisters have been holding things up pretty well. I try to turn, shrug my shoulder, and I think the material has shrunk these past couple of days. I reach around me, turning and spinning. I can't get a hold of the buttons.

The bounty hunter swipes his hand down over his mouth. Stepping forward, he grabs me by the shoulders. "Stop before you hurt yourself."

With my back to him, I glance over my shoulder and suck in a deep breath. One by one, he undoes my buttons.

"Never thought you'd be undressing a woman in a jail cell, now did you?" Maybe it wasn't the best thing to say. He grunts, working his way down through the back of me. "How did you get into this?"

"One of the dance hall girls." And feeling my skin rippling with anxious anticipation, I talk. I keep my voice low, whispering all the dirty details of how I encountered the Brownell brothers.

When the dress falls forward, I hold it close to the sisters. A wall of warmth presses against my back. His hands slide over my shoulders, the dress going down, and I grab it.

"Let it go, Dimples."

And I do. Holding my breath, I tilt my chin and glance back at him. My heart trotting above my lungs. I let my eyes flutter close, waiting.

The bounty hunter steps back, the wall of warmth disappears, and when I open my eyes, he stands with his back turned.

His hands planted on his hips. I duck my head and grab my clothes. My heart goes from a near gallop to a slow walk.

While I dress, he keeps his back to me. I make enough noise to alert another jail break. Nothing.

"You can look now." I pull my curls down over my shoulders. I reach for the dress, but the bounty hunter grabs a hold of my hand. "Leave it."

On the other side of the door, a disgruntled-looking man with a bald spot on his head glares at me. I never caught his name, but I know he's one of the deputies. He watches us go, and outside the roads are muddy with rain and the clouds grow heavy. I can see why the bounty hunter is eager to be on our way.

His destination, though, is about to become altered. There is no way I'm returning to Deadwood with empty pockets and a killer or two on the loose.

13

Outside the sheriff's office, I breathe in the heavy scent of clean air. It's thick, as thick as the clouds hanging above us. I don't question where the sheriff went. Ever since I mentioned to the bounty hunter about Payne taking his position in town too far, the man has a disgruntled expression on his face.

He's got issues. We have this deal between us. I don't ask. He keeps my secrets. Except, it's not so much a secret anymore. Tail Feathers and his people should stay safe with the deal we have with the railroad, but I'm not sure about Chitto anymore. For a brave warrior, his first instinct is to survive. This time, instead of standing and fighting, he ran. I don't blame him. I wish I could have stopped him. The sheriff probably went off to hunt him and the outlaw who caused the breakout.

"Dimples," the bounty hunter says.

When I don't answer him, he says, "Jo," gruffer than before.

"They'll go after him. Chitto. The sheriff will hunt him down. Then what will happen to Tail Feathers and the others? We had a deal." I whirl around, grab his coat edges.

The bounty hunter covers his hands over mine. The

warmth spreading from his palm sends bumps spreading over my skin.

"Chitto is on his own. He's a threat to the tribe. Either way, a renegade is the least of our problems."

"Everything I've done is to protect them."

"Everything?" The bounty hunter lifts my hand. He takes my hand, the ring catching in his fingers. "What's this?"

Those grey eyes of his implore mine.

"It belongs to another woman. She lost it and I'm keeping it for her until I can return it."

Gently, he slips it from my fingers. My breath hitching as it slides the rest of the way off, leaving my finger bare before him. "You shouldn't wear another woman's ring."

"No." I pull my hand from his grasp. I don't suppose I should, I think. Nor should I be with another woman's husband. I blink to keep the emotions of my aching heart at bay. I look at the man the judge declared my husband. The one whose kiss awakens parts of me I didn't know existed. But he's not mine, and it hits me. I never will be his. The bounty hunter will always be married to the wife he lost. The one I can never replace, and I wouldn't want to try.

He stuffs the ring in his shirt pocket and says he'll put it in the safe in the sheriff's office until the woman comes to claim it. Unable to resist, I reach up, straighten the sheriff's star on his breast pocket, and sigh.

"I best go see about the black at the livery."

The bounty hunter gives me a questioning look, far from the hooded gazes that can make butterflies hatch in my stomach.

"Chitto's horse." I rode the black in and allowed my pony to rest. By the look on my husband's face, I have a lot more explaining to do.

"I'll go with you," he says. "I'm not leaving you out of my sight again."

"It's not like I'm going to run away from you. I'll meet you at the livery and I'll show you where I've been staying."

As I go to walk away, he grabs me. "You haven't been staying at the hotel?"

"Hotels cost money and remember, the thieves stole all mine."

He narrows his eyes. "I gave you cash."

"I'm saving it for a rainy day." And is if the sky hears me, a low rumble of thunder emits from the sky. Maybe it came from the bounty hunter as his chest widens and his grip tightens.

"You have been camping out with the renegade?"

By renegade, I hope he means Chitto. "It's not like I haven't ever spent the night in his company."

"Jo," his voice lowers. A glint flashes across the grey in his eyes.

"I'll show you where. Put the ring in the sheriff's safe and I promise I'll wait for you at the livery."

Thankfully, he lets me go, but I can see he doesn't like it. "I won't be but a minute. Stay here. I'll walk with you."

Then the sky crackles and drops of rain grace us once more. It's been the coldest and rainiest summer I've experienced in all my twenty-three years.

"Where's your hat?" he asks.

"I left it back where I've been staying," I admit, purposely not telling him I put it over the dead man's face to keep it from creeping me out when I look at it.

He opens his mouth, about to say something when Sheriff Silver rides up main street with two other men. One of them is tied and slung over a horse. I hold my breath, and the bounty hunter releases my hand. He steps closer, and I'm relieved to see the man isn't Chitto. It's not the outlaw who broke him out either.

"I see you got my message," Silver says to the bounty hunter. "Found this one right where you said I would."

"Wait? You knew where an outlaw was, and you didn't bring him in?" I ask.

"I had more important things to tend to." He looks at me and my face turns hot. "Oh," I say, glancing away, when I glimpse a woman in tan skirts headed down the street. She has a small boy by the hand and her bonnet covers her hair. She's familiar. Then it hits me how I know her.

I saw her at the dancing hall. It's her ring in the bounty hunter's pocket. A boy clings to her skirts. She picks him up, carrying the small tike across the street to the same side as where we're standing. She takes one look my way, then heads away.

"He told me where to find him, so part of the reward I reckon is yours," Silver says to the bounty hunter.

"Keeping my wife safe is reward enough," the bounty hunter says, but I interject. "Isn't he so sweet?" I say in my best drawl. Hanging out with Daphne Davenport and her 'lady-lessons' are coming in handy. Too bad we're no longer friends.

I give the bounty hunter a nudge. "You know you could use that reward money to pay off my bill at the mercantile. I need to settle before we go, anyway."

I try to smile as innocently as possible. The bounty hunter scowls. "Let's step inside and settle up, then."

Glancing again for any signs of the woman and her son, I ask. "Don't you need to take care of him?" I point at the man hung over the horse.

"No matter. He's dead," the sheriff says.

The bounty hunter shrugs, and I have a suspicion the sheriff found the man that way, which is why he's offering to share the reward. I hope it's more than the ten dollars he gave me.

"Yeah, but don't you need to take him to the undertaker's place?" I don't say like the way he made me—or tried to — take the dead body when I brought one in.

The sheriff strokes his chin. "I suppose. Don't want to scare folks. Well, better get it done. You want to come along, and we'll stop at the bank. Can't trust to leave much in my office, not with the state of things as they are. Although," the sheriff says, and I wince, "Your wife cost some damage to my jail."

"Me?"

"Got two escaped prisoners," Sheriff Silver grunts.

"I didn't blow up your jail, and I didn't run, now, did I?"

The bounty hunter puts his hand on my back, gives me a small, but subtle, shove. "You best get what you need for us to be on our way. I'll help the sheriff and see you at the livery." There's a note of warning in his voice, and it makes me smile broader.

"Sure thing." I reach up to tip my hat and forget I don't have it. Instead, I push back my hair and turn on my heel.

I'm stunned a little by the way he left me walk away. I press my hand to my heart, glad to have been able to get away. And even more glad the sheriff came along when he did. Because if he didn't, I might have spilled my own secrets to the bounty hunter. One of them, including how much it hurt to take off that ring. I know it belongs to another woman, but suddenly I can't help wanting one of my own more than anything because I am most certainly in love with my bounty hunter turned sheriff husband.

One thing I will have to confess to the bounty hunter is the lie about having to pay the local mercantile, or will I? Walking in that direction, I figure I might need some supplies and there's got to be a way to buy me more time before the bounty hunter makes me go back to Deadwood. I hope the woman has the answers to helping me find the Brownell Gang. The bounty hunter still has the ring, but if I told him about the woman, then he would have wanted to come with me and spoil my chance to get any information.

My trap might not work this time, but I'm dead set on

catching those robbers. Something tells me Brody Brownell knows a thing or two more about the bounty hunter's past, and I plan on making him sing like a bird. Before, of course, I turn him in for murder and robbery.

I hope the bank in Silver Valley has enough cash inside it by the time I bring those bad boys in hog-tied and draped over the back of their horses.

It's been days, though. I cross my fingers and hope they haven't fled town.

Nearing the mercantile, I step down off the sidewalk to cross the muddy alley. Turning up the collar of my coat, I duck my head against the rain when an arm goes around me and yanks me against the side of a building.

My face is shoved into the rough planked siding. Crying out, I try to fight, kicking back. My boot connects with a shin. A man curses and the steel of his gun jabs into my side. "Stop, Jo. It's me."

I freeze.

"Bounty Hunter?" I spin around.

"You ever going to call me Chord? That's my name, Dimples."

Flabbergasted, I stammer, "But you… But I…" my finger points towards the mercantile. My chances of catching up with Emory's wife are waning.

"I have a better idea," he says, "One where you won't need any supplies and I won't need to worry about you while I track down Brownell."

"But…"

He puts his hand over my lips, ducks his head, and watches the stagecoach pull up down the street.

"If you think for one moment, I'm leaving here on the stage…."

The bounty hunter doesn't give me a chance to finish. "One of these days you'll learn to listen," he says.

I try to yank my arm from him as he pulls me in the stage's direction. I dig in my heels, but the bounty hunter grunts and holds me with both hands. Some folks stare at the window as I scream, but when he says, "Nothing to worry about, folks. Just a husband tending to his wife is all."

Aiming to hit him, the bounty hunter grabs my fist. "Now that's not nice, Mrs. Townes." Those grey eyes of his turn hard and cold. "You can walk and get on that stage, or I can drag you there. Whichever you prefer."

"Neither. I have unfinished business here." His lips turn down into a frown. He's not going to budge. Doing the first thing that comes to mind, I yell, "Who says you're my husband? You see, a ring on this finger?"

The man winces as if I struck him. There's a cloud passing by in his eyes and instantly I regret the words from my mouth. He leans in, nose to nose, and I stare right back at him.

"This wasn't the plan." Never have I ever been so mad I could cry.

"Let's say I changed my mind as you've had a change of heart, wife." No truer words could be told. Except my heart hasn't listened since the day I ran smack into the bounty hunter. "You don't have a heart," I hissed. "If you put me on that stage alone, I won't go home."

"Jo." The bounty hunter yanks me up against him. We're a few inches apart in height, but with my cowgirl boots dangling, we're eye to eye. He grimaces and I can tell he wants to say something more. A few men come laughing out of the shop behind us, bringing the smell of cigar smoke wafting with them.

'What's going on?" Panic erupts in me. This isn't like the bounty hunter.

"Tell me where the body is."

"And you won't put me on the stage?"

He gives this dead pan look. Of course not. An amused

snort came out before I can stop it. "This is how you treat me? We're supposed to be partners." Weren't we? Hadn't Polly claimed that what my father owned should have been hers? Hadn't Earl always said married folk work together? Or was it Ella Mae who told me that?

Right at this moment, it didn't matter. If the bounty hunter thought he could pull a fast one on me, he was mistaken.

"You know what will happen if you send me back alone?" The gambler's face swims in my thoughts like a fish trying to escape a waterfall.

My threat doesn't faze him.

"One day you'll thank me." He looks beyond me and when I try to turn, he twists me around. Before I can blink, I find myself shoved into a stagecoach. The door slams, and from the other side of the curtain, I hear Sheriff Silver say, "You made the right choice."

The man is like a ghost appearing from thin air. I have no doubt he put the bounty hunter up to this plan.

As I reach for the handle, another man across from me lifts the barrel of his gun. "I've been instructed to shoot if you try to get out before we reach our destination, *Mrs. Townes.*"

I push aside the curtain and glare at the bounty hunter. He tips his hat and continues down the street. "What about my pony!"

"I'll miss you, too!" The bounty hunter shouts, and the sheriff adds, "Don't you take your eyes off her for a minute Dougie,"

Slouching back against the inside of the coach, I cross my arms and stare at my jailer. I should have known the bounty hunter would pull something like this on me. I missed my opportunity to question Emory's wife, but sooner or later good ole Dougie would look the other way. None of them had the sense to tie me.

Curling my hands into a fist, I decide it is better this way.

Who needs a dumb ole ring on their finger, anyway? Emory's wife is blessed in more ways than the women knew. Slouching deeper in my seat as the stage shifts. Another man climbs in the driver's seat, and I blow a curl from my face as the stage lurches forward.

14

"You tell the sheriff where you hid that body?"

Ha! As if I would give away my hiding place after he turned a dirty trick on me like this. I'm so angry I could spit. And yes, I know that goes against the lady rules Daphne once gave me. Although, who cares about Daphne Davenport and her lady's rules? We're not friends, not like Ella Mae and I are.

Then there is the bounty hunter. My gut burns with his betrayal. It makes me downright ill. He doesn't want me around. I can take a hint, but what business of it is his for me to go trying to get the town's money back?

It's not like he's not after the money, too. Well, he's after the bounty. A man like Chord Townes doesn't need to worry about where his next meal is coming from or taking care of himself.

He wasn't kidding when he said I was going back to Deadwood. I suppose bailing me from jail, the sheriff probably convinced him he was better off without me, and isn't he, though?

I sigh, remembering the hard set of his jaw and those stone-cold gray eyes. Another shiver slips down my spine recalling the way he looked at me as he opened the door and shoved me inside. Can't blame him, though, can I?

Jo Dean, you fool, I chide myself. You done and got yourself wrapped up worse than a hare with a rattler. I suppose I should have seen this coming, but from the bounty hunter, it slices a girl where it hurts. Right across her heart and I can't help the feelings I have developed for the bounty hunter since the Judge hitched us together.

How will I ever get myself out of this one? It's not enough I screwed up and both the Brownells and the sheriff's prisoner are gone. I dragged Chitto into this, too. The entire tribe is in danger because of my recklessness. Chord didn't have to say it. If I ever thought the man would claim me his actual wife, I blew it.

Feeling deflated, I look across at Dougie. I am not gonna ask how he got his name or put any charm on him to escape. The six-shooter in his hand doesn't look like it's up for any sweet-talking. Turning my head away, I look out beyond the curtain again. The bounty hunter gave my shotgun to the coachman.

"She can have it when you reach Deadwood, and not before. If she tries to open the door or run, shoot her."

My eyes widen. He wouldn't dare! The audacity of the man! Oh Lord, now I *do* sound like Daphne. The coachman yells to his horses and we're off, headed back straight back to Deadwood.

Beside me is a soft man, whose hands haven't seen a day's work and his face as white as a China plate. He sits stiffly beside me. His suit jacket and pants don't have a wrinkle and I can't help wondering where he's come from. Even his aftershave smells expensive.

On the other side of us are two more men, one who looks at me like I'm a prime rib. His pants are clean, and his hair feathered behind his ears. He's got a curl in his lip that makes me glance away. Those yellow teeth could make a girl lose her breakfast. But the other one, Dougie, sits beside him, and pulls his hat down over his face. Dougie has guns strapped on either side of his hips and one hand rests on the nearest weapon. He holds his hat to keep it in place until the horses' pace finds a rhythm.

The bounty hunter better make sure nothing happens to Lulu. I tilt my head back in silent prayer for my precious paint pony. Between Lulu and Shorty, I have little left of my old life. A girl's got to hold on to a few prized possessions in this life, or does she?

Glancing over again at the man beside me, I realize as he tugs on his mustache how familiar his facial features seem. "Excuse me," I say, "I can't help wondering if we've met."

He offers me his hand. "Charles Conway."

Conway. Frowning, I ask, "As in relation to Thomas Conway?"

"I am his son."

I gasp. "You're Daphne Davenport's intended husband."

What a small world. Maybe going back to Deadwood on the stage won't be so bad after all. The price to see Daphne's face when her 'mail-order husband' arrives will be payment enough.

"You are in acquaintance with Miss Davenport?" He pulls back his shoulders. His cheeks go a little red.

"I am."

"Of course, then she must have mentioned me," Charles' chest expands.

"How else would I have known who you are?" Poor sod. Daphne had better of worked her magic on the gambler or considered the hotel owner Jed Warner a good suitor, else she'll be saddled with this softy until death do they part. Maybe I'm wrong, and the two will be a match made in heaven. For their sake, I hope I am.

"Conway. You're with the railroad." The man beside Dougie says. "Why not take the train?"

"They haven't laid the tracks yet between the towns," I say.

"It will take a year at this rate to dig through the mountain. Too slow, if you ask me, but progress is progress," Charles responds.

The last thing on my mind is the railroad. The others talk about Indians, gold, and new laws in the west.

I turn my head, taking in the scenery as the men continue to talk of railroads and politics. Charles puts his hand on my arm as I lean against the side. "I should tell you; your husband has instructed all of us to tie you if necessary to keep you on the stage."

Oh, it doesn't surprise me, it makes me mad, and madder yet because he betrayed me. He hurt my feelings, but I learned a long time ago not to let them show.

Looking at the other three men inside the stage with me, I say, "Let me guess, he also gave one of you the rope?"

Dougie chuckles. While the other two look sympatric to my plight, Dougie keeps his hand near his gun. He won't be needing that rope.

He's looking at me again, his eyes intent on me, and suddenly I want to clutch the side of the coach tighter. It's a day's ride between the two towns, but at some point, the stage will have to stop to let us have a moment to ourselves. I'm hoping for bushes since I didn't see any stage stations on my way here.

The bounty hunter better take care to bring Lulu back to Deadwood with him. I imagine a dead body hanging over Lulu's back with the face of Brody Brownell. One way or another, I am going to find out what that man knows about my husband, who killed Buck and where the town's money, including mine, has gone.

Along the way, I try to express the need to find a bush, but the stagecoach driver is having none of my ploy. The man on the other side of me keeps his hat and continues to sleep while Charles and the other man have no problem conversing. At some point they all fall silent and even the stagecoach has slowed and kept a steady pace. Pulling aside the blinds, the mountains come into view. They make me think of Chitto.

The worst thing Chitto could have done is run from the law. What will happen to Chitto's wife and the tribe if the Cavalry know a renegade is on the loose? I have to find him right after I bring in Brody and his gang for killing Buck and stealing Deadwood's money. If I were a robber, where would I go to hide? Where would I stash my loot until it was safe to spend it?

The bounty hunter would have found the body and taken it to town by now. Next time Mrs. McLoughlin comes to town she'll find out I'm a lair. Now that I think of it, I've seen her in town a few times, and with no children.

A few hours into the ride, I ask, "How long before we stop?"

Dougie opens one eye to squint at me. "We got a way to go yet."

"Perhaps the lady needs a moment of privacy," Charles says. "I know I could."

The other man shakes his head, but Dougie responds first, "There will be a station between here and Deadwood, we'll stop to stretch our legs when we get there. Then the woman and you can have a minute of privacy, as you say, if you need it."

Charles grunts, "You misunderstood me."

I lay my hand on his arm and his gaze goes to my ungloved fingers. I pull my hand away. "He knows what you meant, and yes," I lean toward Dougie, "I could use the bushes if you gander my meaning."

Dougie, having put his pistol away a few miles back, places

his hat back over his face. "Cross your legs, sister. We've got another hour or two before we reach the station."

"That is no way to talk to a lady," Charles says.

Dougie grins, "Who says Mrs. Townes is a lady? I heard she was in the dancing hall and got arrested. Not the first time she's been in jail either, is it Mrs. Townes?"

Charles and the other man both look at me for an answer. Not ashamed, I tell them the truth. "My husband is the sheriff of Deadwood. Of course, I've been to jail."

Dougie snorts.

"Pay him no mind, Mrs. Townes. Some men have no manners when it comes to women. It comes as no surprise why the gentlewomen of the east are so hesitant to come in this direction."

"Dakota Territory isn't for everyone," the man by Dougie agrees. I paid little attention to him. He wears a plain jacket and a wide-brimmed hat. If the man packs any heat, he keeps it concealed, but the way his jaw has a smear of growth on it and his dark eyes are set back more than most, I don't think he'd make a good shot. His boots have scuffs on the sides.

"Mind if I ask what has you heading to Deadwood, Mister?" I inquire.

He inclines his head, a sly grin sneaking on his face, "I've business, Mrs. Townes."

"What kind of business?" Charles asks, not at all apologetic for interrupting.

"I've a prospect on the mountain."

"Interesting," Charles twists his mustache.

"I've a claim in the mountains. The railroad has paid me handsomely for the rights to go through it, not many left up there," I say.

His grin splits open and shows a set of straight white teeth. "I aim to make my fortune."

"I lived in those mountains all my life." Before the railroad and the gambler tried to steal my claim and there's not more than a lick of gold in our mine from all our days of panning, but I don't tell the stranger. "I wish you the best of luck," then I realize, "I don't believe I got your name."

His grin turns into a full-blown smile. "I didn't give it." He holds out his hand across the stage, but just as I'm about to take it, shots and shouts come from the distance. The driver shouts for us all to hold on as he cracks the reins, and the horses take off at a faster speed. I lurch forward and the stranger grabs a hold of me. Pulled on the other side of the coach, the two men keep me between them while Charles Conway grasps both sides of the coach, sliding back and forth to hold his seat.

Suddenly, the horses appear on the sides of the coach. A crack and several more shouts and shots come from outside. A bullet strikes the door and Charles nearly faints.

Dougie pulls out his pistols, using his feet to wedge against the sides to hold steady as he points his gun out beyond the swinging curtains on the side, "Get down!" He growls, shoving me to the floor. Charles follows, and the air is squeezed from my lungs.

"Give me your other gun," the stranger says. I hear nothing but the sounds of the creaking wagon chassis under the stage, the horses' hooves pounding, and the shots embedding into the wood. "I. Can't. Breathe."

Charles does not budge. The stranger tried to help me after I shoved him. Soon the stage hits a bump, and we all end up in a stack in the middle, me on the bottom again. Charles is on top of me with the stranger on top of him. We both push and shove until the larger man is off me. As I'm getting up on all fours and climbing back to my seat, a shot rings out, and the driver takes a dive off the top.

Charles Conway lays between the two seats. "Is he dead?"

None of us have enough time to find out, above sounds of

someone going across the top of the ceiling distract us. Dougie keeps shooting, but then someone shouts 'whoa' and the stage slows. As it comes to a stop, I bend down with Mr. Conway. I can't find any place where he might have been hit, but one thing is for certain: Charles Conway lies at the bottom of the coach, unconscious.

The door wretches open and a man with a hankie over his nose and mouth motion for us to get out. His pistol isn't as big as the bounty hunters, but the way he waves it at us, says he means to use it.

"Ladies first." For the first time, I think the man isn't much of a gentleman.

"Toss your weapons out and stay where you are."

I freeze. That's an odd request for a robber, isn't it? I hold up my hands. Dougie drops his pistols out the door as he's told.

"Now you men, get on out."

Men, not the lady. "You heard him," I say.

Dougie is the first one to exit along with the stranger. "What about him?"

"He dead?" the outlaw asks.

"Yes," I plea on Charles Conway's behalf. I'm pretty sure he is breathing, but what is one lie to keep another alive?

"Get him out of there," the outlaw says to another and for the first time, I see the robber's partner. There are two others outside and another one holding the horses.

"You get him out of there," Dougie says. "You killed him."

The outlaw shoves the barrel of his gun in Dougie's ribs. "You want to say that again?"

"Oh, forget it, Ford, we got what we need. The fellow's dead. Just leave him."

Ford. My heart leaps as fast as the horses were running. It's hard to see with his face covered up, but if this is the same Ford who escaped the prison with Chitto, then...

"Tie them up and leave them. We got to get to the rendezvous point."

"What about the woman?" someone asked.

"She's coming with us." Ford grabs hold of the door of the stage, swings himself up inside to sit across from me. He kicks Charles, and the man doesn't even make a sound. My heart swells for the railroad man's son. And for Daphne.

Ford sits across from me. His gun points in my direction. "Don't try anything or I'll shot."

"Where have I heard that before," I mutter, but decide to keep my mouth shut as he lowers his chin and glares at me.

Several minutes later, the horses are hitched and take off again, leaving Dougie and the stranger tied up at the side of the road. We've got a new driver and new passengers. The back window curtain flaps and I catch glimpses of a horse tied to the rear of the stage and another rider to our left.

"Where are you taking me?" I ask.

Ford doesn't answer, his gun never wavers, and I pray for Charles Conway's sake that he's dead, lest he wakes up and gets us both killed.

15

"You won't be able to get away with this," I tell him. "You should have ditched the stage." I ramble on more nervous than a jackrabbit.

"This here stage is worth more than you'll ever know, sweetheart," Ford chuckles. He's a rough-looking cowboy, with deep lines in his face. I can't tell if his tan is from staying out in the sun too long or not bathing. Either way, I don't care to find out. We ride for what feels like forever until I hear the driver shout for the horse to slow and come to a stop.

Ford is the first to exit. "Don't try running. A bullet in your leg won't kill you, but it'll hurt something terrible."

The man should still be locked up in Silver Valley's jail. My stomach sinks thinking about Chitto. Where is he? I'm too afraid to ask, but as I stumble out of the coach. A set of arms catches me, and I look into the eyes of a familiar face.

"Chitto," I breathe a sigh of relief.

He leans in and whispers, "Did you really think I would leave you?"

My heart skitters to a stop. He still loves me. He came back for me. But then Ford yanks me from Chitto. "She ain't yours," he grumbles, then shouts out orders to the others. "Wait here for the signal."

"What's happening?" I direct my question to Chitto. He's as tight-lipped as a bear trap.

"Stay here," Ford tells Chitto. "They'll send out the others to inspect the goods. You'll get your share." Then he grins at me. "And you'll get what's coming to you."

Those words stir a sickness in my stomach, and I try not to let the bile rise in my throat. "I'm unarmed. Surely, you wouldn't harm a lady."

He laughs and pulls me along. We're at a stagecoach station. There's a house with a long porch and a barn to the right. Men step out from the barn, and I think I know at least one of them. It's Emory McLoughlin. He tips his hat as he saunters towards the dusty outlaws around the stage. What would they want with the stage, anyway?

A woman in a tan dress steps out on the porch, and it takes me a moment to catch my breath. Mrs. McLoughlin. I saw her at the mercantile. How did she get here?

Brody Brownell and his brother Irwin step on either side of her.

"I brought the girl. Now pay up?"

"Our business isn't done yet," Brody grins, tips his hat and says, "Nice to see you again, Mrs. Townes."

"What's this all about?" I glance around, trying to find Chitto.

"We got it!" A shout comes from the stage. A man atop the coach holds up a few bags in the air.

"I'll see they get their split, then we'll make it back to our next stop on time." Irwin scratches his chin. "You sure you want to bring her along?"

"You promised Emory and I could stay here," Mrs. McLoughlin pleas. I can see the hint of fear in her eyes. She steps off the porch in my direction, but Body grabs hold of her.

"Let Emory handle it; you'll get your cut when the deal is done." He levels those dark eyes on her. She gives him a curt nod and steps back inside. "I'll grab my bonnet."

Where are the children? Inside, I glimpse two men, and a woman all tied up on chairs from the eating area.

"You mind telling me what's going on?" I muster the courage to ask.

"You'll find out soon enough." Brody says.

"This wasn't part of our deal," Ford speaks up, his face red at the ears.

"You'll go to Deadwood like we planned," Brody pulls out his gun faster than Ford.

"There ain't no going back!" Ford seethes. "I told you I don't want any part of this plan."

"I broke you out, didn't I?" Brody's eyes narrow. I take a step out of the line of firing. Another one to be sure I'm clear, but Brody cocks his gun and says, "Don't take another step further, Mrs. Townes." My name comes off his lips like soured milk.

I push back one of my curls as sweat forms under the sisters and I take a deep breath as to keep my heart from bursting between them.

"You're crazy to go back there. Let's take the money and run."

"We stick to the plan. Unless your like Ebbi," he says.

I try to swallow, my lips suddenly dry. I keep my eyes on his gun.

"Then shoot me, but we both know you need me."

Why else had they gone to Silver Valley to bust Ford from the Iron Horse? But why go back? Why return to Deadwood? None of this made sense and the confusion must've shown on my face. Brody laughed. "We've got this one here and the Indian. You think you're not disposable?"

"Like you disposed Ebbie?"

At the sound of her brother's name, Mrs. McLoughlin returned with Emory. "What about Ebbie? Where is he? You said he was alive." She looks right at me, those eyes filled with hope, tear me in two. Even if my life depends on it, I cannot lie. I glance away and the lot of them go into an argument. Chitto has a long rifle in his hand. He tilts his head and I take off running.

I don't make it far when something slams into me from the back. Falling, my face plants into the dirt, and before I can think of getting up, pain explodes at the side of my head. Funny, this isn't how I thought getting shot would feel.

A stampede of wild horses run over my head. It pounds and throbs as I open my eyes. Blurry at first, I blink and blink until I can make out a haze of figures. It's dark, which makes focusing worse. I moan, not meaning to, but I can't reach my head to hold it still as my hands are tied behind my back. The world spins, or maybe I'm tilting, and there's a campfire nearby. I hear the angry snapping of wood inside flames. Some kind of meat roasts above the fire on a spit and for a moment I feel nauseas.

Men are talking, one man is more agitated than the others.

"You think I busted you out of the iron horse for a woman?"

Didn't I hear this conversation before? Am I dead and reliving the last few moments of my life? But no, I tilt my head to the side, realizing I'm tied to a chair. My vision comes back. Slowly, I see the flare of a woman's skirts. Tan. Trying to lift my chin without losing the contents of my stomach, I squint. It's not a campfire, but a fireplace.

And I'm tied to the back of a solid wood chair

"I thought we had a job to do?" another voice grumbles.

"We do."

I recognize the last voice. It's Brody Brownell.

"Just as soon as the woman tells us where to find Ebbi."

"Forget Ebbi. He's dead."

A finger hooks under my chin, lifting it as I come eye level with Emory McLoughlin. Behind him stands his wife, her hands twisted in the gown I spotted her wearing earlier. "Where's Ebbi?"

I swallow down the bile in my throat.

"Please." The woman pleads. "Don't tell them. They're gonna kill him."

"I'm going to kill you in a minute, if you don't keep your trap shut," Irwin Brownell grabs the woman by the arm.

Emory scowls. "Take your hands off my wife."

We're in a two-room cabin and beyond the men a door hinges open enough for me to see a little face peering through. Something tells me we left the stagecoach station a while ago.

"Tell us where Ebbi is," Irwin demands.

"Think I'm stupid?"

If they don't kill me, I'm sure the bounty hunter is wishing he'd left me locked in that jail.

"Ebbi's alive, you said so?" the woman whispers, and I notice for the first time how pale she is compared to the men. Every once in a while, she glances at the door.

"Let me go and I'll take you to him." I wince, hating that I'm giving false hope to the woman, but determined to stay alive.

"She lies." Chitto's voice comes out of the darkness. I can make out his outline in the corner by the window. His rifle perched as he watches for intruders.

"I'm with him. She's lying."

"What she got to gain by lying?" Mrs. McLoughlin says.

"The same any woman does," says Brody, leaning back and playing with the chamber of his gun.

"His body is nothing but food for the forest," Chitto says. "Move on with this plan. Your former friend is gone."

"Shouldn't you be out patrolling?" I grumble. All the plans I have aren't worth a penny or another thought. Surely, by now, the bounty hunter would know I didn't make it to Deadwood. What of Dougie and the stranger? Oh Lord, Mr. Conway! "Where's Charles?"

We left him in the stagecoach. How will I ever explain this to Mr. Conway? What will happen to our contract with the railroad? I groan inwardly, as I figure this is one more thing for Daphne to hold against me.

What would Ella Mae say about all this?

"I'll check on our fat friend." Chitto slips from the cabin on the other side of the door, but then I see his shadow out the window. He won't leave, I hope. And I pray he doesn't go far.

If by 'fat friend' he refers to Charles Conway, then maybe God has been riding along with me all this time.

"You're going to take us to him, alright," Emory glares at me. "And you'd best not be lying about him being alive."

"If Chitto says he's dead, then he's dead. You'd know if you'd done the job right." Ford, my kidnapper, grunts.

Emory gives him a deadly look and glances back at his wife. "I didn't do it."

"Brody did," Irwin grins. "And I plan to put another bullet in him to finish the job. Seems my little brother can't even do that right these days."

"Then which one of you shot the rancher in the posse?" I ask.

"Could have been anyone of us, Darlin'," Brody says. "But I'll say Irwin has the trigger finger out of all of us."

"Brody…" Irwin hisses, "I'll show you my trigger finger."

"That's enough," Emory whines. "What do we do about the woman now that we've got her? She wasn't part of the plan." He glowers at Brody.

"Oh, but she is," Brody, tilts back and slams the chamber of his gun closed. "No one in town will question Mrs. Townes heading in the bank to make a deposit."

"Deposit?" I blurt, "You done already robbed the bank." And took my money with it.

They all grin. "Ever play duck, duck, goose?" Brody asked.

I shake my head.

"Shame, but trust me when I say you're the goose."

I am a cooked goose for sure. As I listen to Brody lay out the plan, my arms ache and my head throbs. "We're going to walk right into the bank and give their money back?"

"Sort of," Irwin chuckles.

"I'll be opening a new account," Emory's wife whispers. "What if this plan doesn't work?"

"It's not my plan," Brody says, then frowns when he admits he's not the mastermind.

Who is?

I check for Chitto again, but he's disappeared. I listen as they unfold tomorrow's events and think to myself, how could I have ever been such a fool? Where's the bounty hunter when I needed him?

Something told me I'd have to get out of this one on my own.

16

We'd ride inside the stage until we got to Deadwood. Once there, Brody and his crew would let me go after they'd finished their business. Or at least, that's what they told me, but I didn't believe them. Who believes someone who kills and robs for a living?

Mr. And Mrs. McLoughlin ride across from us inside, while up on top the stage, driving it, sits Irwin. Few people would recognize him, even with the wanted posters hanging around. He shaved the growth off his chin and kept his handkerchief in his pocket instead of covering his face like his photos. The man had eyes as large as an owl, so big, if someone looked hard enough, they'd would be the most prominent thing to recognize about him. On either side of us rode Ford and Chitto. My gut burned with his involvement. Several times I attempt to speak with him, and in his own language, but he looks the other way. How could I help the man if he wouldn't talk to me?

Then there's poor Mr. Conway's son, Charles. They rolled him right out of the stage and left him at the station. Lord, please don't make me the one who will have to deliver the bad news. Kill me first, okay?

I'd already experienced the wrath of one Daphne Davenport over a broken leg in trying to save her life. Who knows what kind of story or relation she would conjure up with her lady-like wails and batting lashes to cause me more strife over another thing that wasn't my fault?

But she would and could blame me. What difference would it make? Once I got out of this mess, and I pray I do so, alive, I plan to pack my sorry self up and head back to the mountain where I won't be a burden to anyone else. If anyone missed me, it would be Ruby. And a part of me sags with the heaviness of telling her goodbye. And Ella Mae, she'd already gone out to the ranch with her husband, Lincoln. She'd understand. She had to understand, because right at this moment, I am convinced this would be the best for all parties involved. I'm as sure as it is Thursday, the Brownell Gang won't let me live, or if they did, what was about to happen would land me back in jail, and this time as a framed individual, or worse. Everyone in town would think I'd conspired with the robbers.

"Remember when the stage pulls in, you two grab your suitcases and head for the hotel. Ford will grab the satchel and wait for Anabel to come back out with her purse, and they'll head to the bank," Brody goes over the plan for what feels like the hundredth time. My head has a knot the size of Texas where I smacked it on a rock when I fell.

"Make the deposit," he says to Anabel, "Then you'll go on back to the hotel where we'll meet you later. You and our guest will stay there the night, then in the morning, you and her will walk back to the bank, make another deposit. This time she'll do it." Brody looks at me.

"I never said I would go along with this plan." It makes little sense to me. I think when I fell and hit my head, it rattled something loose in my brain. I can't seem to think straight. Who ever heard of a robber putting money back in the bank?

"You'll go along if you want nothing bad happening to your friend," Emory glances out the window.

"Besides," Brody slides closer, his thigh presses against mine, the hard edge of his six-shooter jabs me. "You don't want to find out what happened to your husband's first wife, now do you?"

"Actually, I do," I say.

Brody's eyes mirror the shock I have at saying the words out loud. "How is it, you know?"

Emory smirks. "Anabel, love, you'd best get comfortable," he tells his wife. We're about to hear it all over again.

She looks at him with scorn. I guess she hasn't gotten over the night at the dance hall. Several times, now, I want to mention her ring, but I can see she's got a bone to pick with me, too. Guilt over the whereabouts of her brother's dead body keeps my lips sealed. It would only add fuel to the flames.

"It's a good thing we've got a little way to go yet this morning until we get to Deadwood," Anabel says. "And with any chance, Ebbi will show up and we can all go to the claim together."

Emory gives his wife an elbow to the ribs, and she gasps. I guess she let something important slip. What would a bunch of robbers want with a claim? Shouldn't they have hightailed it and been halfway outside of Dakota Territory by now?

The stretch of silence bothers me. "So, you were saying? Obviously, you know the bounty hunter. Were you the one who killed his wife?"

A girl has a right to voice her suspicions.

"The bounty hunter, as you call him, couldn't shoot a tin can off a fence until our Pappy taught him." Brody leans against the side of the coach, lifts a leg and pulls his hat down on his lap. My hat still rests on a dead man and my fingers inch to do the same.

"You were friends?" I ask.

"We grew up together. Bet Chord likes you calling him the bounty hunter. Feeds his ego right nice."

"Stop it, Brody," Anabel chides. "We all know he's coming for you." She sounds happy at the prospect.

"Oh, he's coming for me alright. I stole away the one thing he could get back." Brody smirks, his eyes glazed with the past.

"His wife," it comes out in a mere whisper.

"His livelihood," Brody looks over at me. "Don't need no wife and a bunch of rug rats to race after." He points his look at Anabel, then at Emory. She scoots closer to her husband. "We never saw eye to eye when it came to the law."

"But you knew her?" I ask, scooting a little closer to the door.

"A local girl. Daughter of a Calvary man. He tell you about wearing the uniform?"

I stare at him, too afraid of admitting how little I know of the bounty hunter. But one thing stands out. I understood why the robbers had uniforms, old and tattered. Brody and Irwin wore theirs, most times. Irwin exchanged to drive the stage. Brody wouldn't part from his, I could see it in his poise. He wore it as he did his pride. The killing had gone to his mind. "Some of us have weaker stomachs than others," Brody says and Emory cuts him off. "There are ladies present."

"You were saying," I gave Emory and Anabel a look. Nothing would stop me from finally knowing what happened to the bounty hunter's first wife. I needed to understand why he behaved the way he did. I clutch my skirt and wait for Brody to tell me.

"We met in the Calvary. Fool would have got himself dead if Pappy hadn't taught him to shoot." He said that already, but I bit my lip and waited.

"They had a falling out," Emory supplies, and Brody grunts. "He had a lot of nerve coming after me for all I did for him."

"And what exactly was that?"

If looks could kill, I wouldn't make it to Deadwood. I lean back against my side of the stagecoach.

"I killed his wife," Brody leans toward me. "You want me to tell you how?"

I'd asked for it. My stomach quivers and my palms get sweaty. "You?"

He licks his lips and leans a little closer.

"Brody," growls Emory.

"Please." Anabel covers her ears. "I don't want to hear this again."

Brody straightens, glancing out the window and his grin turns deadly. "Then I suppose you'll have to wait and hear it from your husband." He rasps on the ceiling of the stage. "What's taking so long?"

Chitto rode up beside the stage, peering in at me and me at him. I press a hand to my stomach, afraid I might toss my cookies. This was one ride I couldn't wait to end.

Anabel reaches over, takes my hand, and whispers, "It'll all be over soon." Her eyes deplore me. I squeeze back, the comfort of someone caring enough.

Not long after I spot the buildings and hear the sounds of the blacksmith hammering on his anvil in his forge, we pass the horses in the corral. I think of Lulu. The bounty hunter better have taken good care of her until I can get her back again.

We stop in front of the hotel, where Jed Warner stands to greet those getting off the stage. My insides tighten with fear I'd see Daphne or one of the other ladies in town who despises me.

"Don't try running off," Brody hooks me back by grabbing

my arm. "If anyone asked, you lost your horse and had to hitch a ride home."

As planned, Emory and Anabel get out, take their bags, and follow the hotel manager inside. He gives me a second glance and I smile to ease the swirling of my insides. Leave it to this morning for the gambler to come strutting out of the cafe with none other than Eva and Emma Swanson on each arm. A little fury builds inside me at the site, but of all the moments to run into the man, I thank the Lord for his timing.

"Darlin'," The gambler spreads out his arms, forgetting about the ladies holding onto them. "You're back."

Eva and Emma Swansons are twin sisters who own the bathhouse here in town. They have golden locks and curves for miles that could lead a man south faster than Reverend Carter could redeem him.

"Don't pretend you missed me," I tell him.

"Why, hello there," Eva Swanson is the shorter of the two sisters. She wears her hair down over her shoulders while she keeps her bustle pinned up in the back. "I don't believe we've met."

"Well, I surely know you," Brody winks at Emma and the woman feigned any interest. While the twins step away from the gambler to entice Brody, I move towards him, but then Irwin jumps down from the coach. He presses his gun against my back where no one in front of me can see it.

"I believe we have business awaiting you in the hotel," Irwin says.

"I'll wait here for you," I try to sound polite. "Mr. Weston is an acquaintance of mine. I'm sure he wouldn't mind walking me to the boarding house. It's not much on the other side of the Swanson's place."

Emma gives me the eye and I'm sure the woman has claws, but enough class to keep them to herself around a bunch of eligible men. Well, any man to the Swanson sisters is deemed eligible when they step inside the bathhouse. I shudder to keep my judgmental mind from getting me in trouble. It's not my place to judge them. They'll have to deal with their life deeds to the man upstairs all on their own.

"You forgot. Your husband made me promise to deliver you to the hotel. He said for you to wait for him here."

"Did he really?" the gambler asks. "I wouldn't think that would be a wise idea."

"No, indeed not," I agree.

Eva Swanson has left the gambler to tap her finger on Brody's arm. She walks her fingers up his dusty jacket. "You'd be better off coming over to our place first, isn't that right, sister?"

Emma tilts her head, not yet ready to give up her place by the gambler. "By all means, we'd love to see you later." She pauses, biting her lip for a minute before she says, "I love a man in uniform."

Brody promises to find them later, and Irwin offers me his arm. "I wouldn't want the bounty hunter to come after me for not delivering you safe and sound, as promised."

I bit back a laugh. Those green eyes of the gamblers implore me to sound the alarm, but then he grins his silly grin, dimples and all, and takes up the Swanson sisters on either arm. "Dinner tonight," he says. "I'll meet you here at the hotel."

"Yes, of course," I say, and he frowns. "Gentleman," he and the Swanson sisters make their way, and Irwin turns to me as they go with the barrel of his gun still rammed against my ribs. "Think you're smart," he says.

"Smarter than you," I mutter back.

By then, Anabel emerges from the hotel. A sigh of relief escapes me as Jed Warner doesn't come with them.

"Excuse me. Driver," Anabel waves at Ford. "I believe I forgot one of my bags."

Ford pulls out the bag in question as Emory stands in the lobby in a deep discussion with Jed Warner. I notice he changed into a suit and Anabel wears a green frock instead of her tan dress.

"Thank you so much. You don't, by chance, know where the bank is? I'm afraid I need to take care of some pressing business."

"Isn't your husband taking you?" I ask.

She waves me off with a nervous giggle. "Oh, he'll catch up soon enough. I wouldn't want to interrupt him."

"This way, ma'am," Ford glares at me as he assists Anabel. Together, they head for the bank. A carpet bag swings from Anabel's arm and Ford carries it for her. It dawns on me as I watch them go. The carpet bag has the money, or some money in it.

"Let's get you settled in the hotel," Brody says.

My mind spins with possibilities and locks on one more suspect.

"That's a bad idea," I tell them. "I can't walk into the hotel or stay there."

"Why not?" Irwin asks.

"I'm not welcome here anymore."

Brody whistles, "You just might be my kind of woman."

Irwin gives him a shove. He takes my arm and puts his gun away before anyone can see it. "Why didn't you tell us that before?"

"You didn't ask. Besides, it would look suspicious for me to stay at the hotel when I live at the boarding house here in town."

Brody nods, "Make sense."

"Now what do we do?"

"Take her around back when Emory and Anabel get back. We can sneak her into their room for the night."

"Or you could let me go. You really don't need me," I say.

"That's where you're wrong." Ford comes walking down the boardwalk from behind us. He leans in and whispers something to Irwin.

"The last thing we need is Chord Townes getting in the way of things," Irwin says.

"He won't be," I try to assure them. "Why do you think he put me on the stage? He's out looking for you. All of you." And he should have gotten on his horse and rode with me to Deadwood instead of trying to be the lone ranger he likes to be.

"Let's stick with the plan," says Brody, holding out his arm for me. "Shall we Mrs. Townes."

My stomach grumbles. I haven't had a bite since the day before. I hope these outlaws plan includes something to do with food, because I get mighty hangry when I am not fed.

"You boys sure you don't want a wet your whistle now that you've gotten to town?"

The gambler's saloon is the last place I ever want to go, but if it will keep this scheme of the robbers drawn out a little longer, I'm willing to make the sacrifice.

"It's too early in the day," Irwin adjusts his hat. He instructs Ford to find Chitto and the pair of us head around the back of the hotel. "What if someone sees me?"

Ordinarily, I'd hope they would, but the thought of running into Daphne Davenport or her father has my steps faltering. It doesn't matter that I know who the mastermind is behind it all. Now I need to find a way to prove it.

Where is Deputy Payne when you need him?

17

As soon as we make it into the hotel, my hands are tied. Again. Anabel brought sandwiches and a few apples in her bag, and I notice the carpeted bag has everything except for the town's money in it.

She lays her bonnet on the bed and sits on the corner as I munch on an apple. She also brought a jug of water and as I eat, I can tell she wants to say something, but Emory comes and stretches out on the bed.

I hope they don't expect me to sleep in this chair for the night or for the three of us to share a bed. Luckily, I'm sitting near a window, and while I listen to voices below the porch roof of the hotel, I can't see anyone underneath it.

A few hours into the setting sun, Emory leaves Anabel and me alone. She orders tea and supper delivered to our room.

"It would be a lot easier if I wasn't tied," I try to convince her to let me use my hands. She looks at me and frowns. "You lied. My brother's dead. Why should I trust you?"

"Because I am a victim in all this, just like you," I say. "You have to know what your husband is doing is wrong. You said yourself he isn't like the rest of them."

"Emory ain't never killed anyone." Anabel sighed. "It's all Brody and Irwin's doing."

"And your brother?" I ask.

"He went along with Emory and look where it got him." She sniffles, pacing the floor. "How long does it take for tea?"

She would pay dearly for it, but when you're spending someone else's dime, what did it matter?

"You could turn him in, get the reward money, and then you and Emory could have a good life. You have children, right?"

Anabel plants her hands on her hips. "Two boys," and she touches her stomach, "and another growing inside."

"What's it like?" I ask, having wondered a time or two about motherhood. I can't say I'm destined to be a mother or a good one, but the thought of not having the opportunity has me yearning for a chance. I don't even know I'd make a good mother, having come from the likes of Polly. She abandoned me when I was younger, left me with Earl, and didn't look back until my father was dead and she thought there would be something in it for her.

Anabel smiles, that dreamy smile one gets when they are envisioning a happy future. I've felt that way a time or two thinking of white picket fences and the bounty hunter.

"You love them so instantly; you'd do almost anything for them. You wait and see," she says to me. "One day, you and your husband will make a few babies of your own."

"You really think Brody will let me go after what he did to the bounty hunter's first wife?"

Her dreamy expression lifts, and the reality of our situation hardens her features. "He said he would."

"But you don't trust him either," I finish for her.

Her frown deepens. "It ain't right what Brody did. Chord was only doing his sworn duty." She turns away and paces a few steps on the other side of the bed. "He likes you. Emory said so. Otherwise, he wouldn't have kept you along with us this long."

"Unless he is planning to use me against my husband." How many times could a man lose a wife? Would it hurt the bounty hunter to lose me? I liked to think it would.

"Once this is all over, we'll be gone. He'll leave and won't come back. None of us will, and we'll have a new life. We're starting over. Brody and Irwin are going far away, not where the Calvary can catch them or any other man. They'll be free, and Emory and I'll have everything we ever dreamed of having. Ebbie, too." Her voice flatters.

"I'm sorry," I say when someone knocks on the door.

Anabel gives me a look and whispers, "Don't say anything or do anything that will get us both in trouble." She backs up, watching me. I place my tied hands down between my legs and nod. It wouldn't surprise me to see one man outside the door. Instead, Minnie comes in carrying a tray. My jaw unhinges, and she gives me a polite smile. There are so many things I want to say to her. Like, what is she doing working here at the hotel than scrubbing backs at the bathhouse? But I don't. I clamp my mouth shut before it gets me in trouble. Any place is better than the Swanson Sisters' Bathhouse, and I'm happy to see her out of that place. I remember the last time she did my hair all fancy. And I can't say I'm relieved that maybe the bounty hunter won't go there anymore. I once caught him with Minnie at the bathhouse, innocent as he claimed. I still didn't like it.

Slowly, Minnie walks in and puts the tray on the table in front of me. "It's good to see you again, Mrs. Townes. Will Mr. Townes be joining you on this stay?"

The way she says it puts me on alert. Anabel raises her chin, her hands clasped together. I can't blow this. I still need to talk to her. When I reach up, I remember my hands. Anabel's eyes widen, but I slip them back down under the pleats of my riding skirt. "No. He's still out chasing those bank robbers. This here is a new acquaintance, Mrs. Anabel...."

Anabel cuts in before I use her real married name with "Fender. My husband and I just got into town on the stage. We're looking to settle on one of the claims on the ridge soon." She rambles and I keep smiling at Minnie as the former bathhouse maid nods. Her dark hair twisted and braided around in a bun at the nape of her neck. She tilts her head as she listens. "Well, I wish you the best. Be careful, though, they haven't caught those killers that robbed the bank. Don't you worry, Chord Townes is the sheriff here, and he always gets his man." Minnie glances at me. Those long lashes flutter for a moment, and she grins.

"Oh, I've been to the bank, the manager is helping my Emory and I open an account and handle purchasing our new place. Seems too nice a town for outlaws to get away with anything here." Anabel moves toward the table with the tea.

"Would you like anything else?" Minnie glances my way again and I tilt my wrist for a second. She glances over at Anabel. "A knife perhaps? These steaks can sometimes get tough. I notice they didn't put any on the tray."

They do smell delicious and my stomach grumbles at the same moment. Anabel sees Minnie at the door. "We'll be just fine. It's so awful nice of Mrs. Townes to have a private meal with me, isn't it? All the traveling of the day has plum made me exhausted from wanting to dine in the dining room this evening. She's been such a wonderful companion on this trip and so helpful."

Minnie raises a brow, and I can tell what the maid is thinking. I mouth for her to find Payne, but she shakes her head as Anabel practically shoves her out the door.

Then she locks it and turns. Sagging against the door for a moment, Anabel sighs and pats her hair. "You did good."

Better than her, if I say so myself. The woman is a Nervous Nelly, but I thank God he sent Minnie to our room.

Anabel sits across from me. "You are taking this well. I really appreciate it. It is the least you could do after what happened to my brother."

I raised my hands up. "Would you mind? It would make eating much better?"

Anabel shook her head. "I can't, but I'll cut your steak if you need help." Spoken like a true mother. I glance out the window, catch a familiar looking dark-haired maid lifting her skirts up from the mud and hightailing it across the street.

"You knew that woman?" Anabel asks, reaching over and cutting my steak for me. They might not have given me a knife, but Anabel had one on her person. I wouldn't ask why.

I'd been bidding my time as I try to figure out what I should do next. Somehow, I need to see Brody in jail, along with Emory and Irwin. I didn't know though, which one for certain killed Buck Dawson, and I was sure Brody shot Ebbie. Maybe I could use that to my advantage.

Picking up my fork, I said, "I've seen her around. I think she cleans the rooms here in the hotel." Minnie has hair styling skills. I thought of my hair and how I need to put it in a better braid as all the curls are springing all over the place on my head.

"You've stayed here? I thought you lived here in town?"

"I do. I live at the boarding house with…" I pause, not wanting to give this woman too much information. "With my husband."

"Brody Brownell isn't a good man." Anabel pours us both a cup of tea to go with our steaks. I couldn't complain, these steaks are at least a dollar a piece at the diner.

"Was he ever?" I ask.

"War does that to people, but from what Emory says, the man was always down right jealous and mean of others. Irwin at least has some sense in him. It was Irwin's idea when Brody first came to him with this scheme of his. I don't believe for a minute it's Brody's idea like he wants us to think," Anabel says.

"Whose idea do you think it is?" Anabel opens her mouth then hurriedly stuffs a piece of steak into it. I don't blame her. My eyes nearly roll back into my brain at the taste. I haven't had beef in the longest time, and I'm not counting the roasts I've been served these past weeks. I moan at the mouthwatering bliss of a well-cooked steak. We eat for a few minutes in silence. When I'm finished with my steak, I ask again, and Anabel shakes her head. She either doesn't know or won't tell me.

I ask about her boys. She has two. She tells me they're seven and four, and she rests her hand so lovingly on the round of her stomach it makes me ache for a little one of my own. "This one will come right before winter. We should be settled in our new home by then."

"Where are your boys?" I ask.

She takes a sip of tea. "My sister has them and she and her husband and their littles will join us in a few weeks. Emory and Pope have talked of starting their own lumber yard for years. We'll finally see it come true. No more quarry work or," her voice lowered, "working outside the law."

"How does this have to do with robbing the bank?" I ask, "I'm confused. They robbed the bank, killed a man, almost killed the sheriff, and now you all are putting the money back?"

"Don't make no sense at all." Anabel offers me more tea and I decline. "That's what I told them, but what do I know? I'm just a woman."

My eyes narrow. "Never underestimate yourself, Anabel. I'm sorry you and your brother got involved with this. If you could tell me what's going on, maybe I could help."

Anabel's back stiffens. "I think you have helped enough."

She blinks back tears. "What kind of person lies about another person's death? Did you even really see him?"

She has me there. "Yeah. I saw him, and if you help me out of this, I'll tell you where."

"How do I know I can trust you?"

"You can't. How can you ensure Brody won't kill me?" The steak in my stomach freezes mid-digestion.

She crosses her arms and gives me a good long look. "Fine. I can't. So, we're even, but I want to know where you saw my brother."

"I'll do better. I'll tell you where he is and even take you to him."

Hope flickers in her eyes and I can't afford to put it out with the truth. She has to know the truth in her heart. Without seeing the body, the doubt still lingers in her gaze. It makes me wonder if Ebbie Fender knew the Lord? Would his sister be content in knowing he walked with Jesus? I didn't dare ask, but I quietly pray for him.

"No one would suspect us bringing back the money. They cleaned the bank out, so the bank is calling in the mortgages on a bunch of land owners. The bank takes the land and can resale it. We put the money, part of the money in the bank, use it to buy our land, and none the wiser."

"What about the people you stole from?" I ask, shock rippling through me as it never occurred to me. Not even while I listened to them all this time make their plans about putting money in the bank and going back to Deadwood.

Brody's visit to Payne comes to mind. Does the good deputy of Deadwood know of this plan? Has he been in on it the whole time?

"The town will make more money," Anabel continues. "The tracks are coming through and there is money in the railroad. They bring it from the east. Besides, the only portion going in is for Emory and I. Irwin and Brody have hid their share."

"What about the other guys?"

"Oh, Ford will go with Brody and Irwin. He's a killer. Meanest of them all. He shot some sheriff and then he got caught by the posse after shooting one of them down. He's probably the one who killed the clerk in Cripple Creek."

As I listen, I store away this information for later. Was it Ford who killed Buck? And I'd stood by while he escaped. My stomach twists and I take the last sip of my tea to calm it.

"Where did they stash the money? Do you know?"

Anabel leans in, hesitates for a moment, then says, "They've been stashing it in the stagecoach, under the seats. They take a little out here and there and deposit it in the other banks using alias names. Smart, right?"

"Real smart," I say. Too bad Anabel isn't too smart by telling me.

"Yep, then this other guy, this silent partner," Anabel waves her hand as she doesn't believe he exists, "He somehow gets his share this way, too. He's some sort of investor, according to Brody. Going to buy the entire mountain and own the entire town."

The only investor I can think of is David Davenport. I wouldn't put it beneath him either. Daphne once told me her father invested almost everything they had into the railroad. Could he come up with extra funds to buy out people's homesteads and claims? Or was he focusing on the town? Daphne had also said they were going to buy a place, didn't she? Or was it rent? Either way, I didn't trust Davenport not to be the silent partner.

Long after Anabel laid atop her bed and snored softly, my mind wouldn't shut down. Not that I plan to sleep, anyway. My wrists are tied, making it hard to get comfortable. Anabel hasn't taken any other measures to keep me in the room. I could unlock it and walk out. For a woman who doesn't trust me, she left me with a lot of options.

The meal tray had been placed out in the hall. I crept over to the door and unlocked it. Slowly, opening it, I look out and catch my breath.

"You need something, Mrs. Townes?" Emory McLoughlin stands outside the door.

"I—I needed to use the water closet."

"Where's Anabel?"

"I didn't want to wake her." I close the door and step out into the hall. "Since you're out here, would you mind walking me?"

Emory tips back his hat, his hand resting on the gun strapped to his hip, and he walks past me. He opens the door, peers into the dark room, hears his wife snoring, and closes it gently.

"This way." He takes me by the arm, none so gently.

On our way to the water closet, I mark this escape route off my list of possibilities. Inside the room, I do my business and think of Plan B. There are no windows in the water closet. Back down the hall, Emory waits for me to go inside.

"You're not going out with the others tonight?" I ask.

"A man has to keep an eye on his wife," Emory says, and I get his meaning. He's got to make sure I don't escape.

Back inside the room, I don't kick off my cowgirl boots, but go to the table by the window. Anabel made sure I didn't have access to a knife. It doesn't stop me from fiddling with the window. As it raises, Anabel yawns and says, "Where are you?"

I hurry over to the bed. "Just came from the water closet. Emory took me. No alarm."

"Oh. Alright then." She lays back down and settles her head on the pillow. "Tell him to come in. I miss him."

"I'll let him know." But she's back to snoring and I tip-toe back to the window. The open window allows the sounds of the saloon to travel through the air. I wonder if the gambler came looking for me or got too caught up with his business on a night like this.

I can smell the dampness of another storm heading for us. Something's riding on the wind and I can feel the coldness of it across my skin.

Looking down, I sigh. There is no way I can slip through the window without falling and breaking my neck.

Think Jo! What's a cowgirl to do?

18

Sometime during the night, Emory comes in, sits in a chair, and props his feet up on the table. It's not one of the most expensive rooms in the hotel, but with the price of steak, they had to make adjustments somewhere. I give it to them. They're not the kind to splurge with other people's money.

I almost feel bad for them. The Iron Horse is no place to raise a baby.

When morning comes, so does the mist of rain. It won't stop until it drowns us. Pretty soon Deadwood will become nothing but one large watering hole if mother nature doesn't cut us all some slack.

Anabel moans and dashes for the nearest water closet. I quirk a brow at Emory, who doesn't move. "You gonna go after her?"

Slowly, he rises. "She's been in the family way before. She won't be long."

He reaches for my hands, pulls out a knife from his boot, and pauses under my ropes. "Don't try anything."

"What makes you think I'm gonna?"

The rope falls to the floor. "Brody needs you. I'd hate to

have to kill you."

"You're not a killer. You didn't shoot the sheriff. You didn't kill Ebbie, and you didn't kill that rancher chasing after you in the posse. You're not going to harm a woman."

"I suggest you don't go trying to find out. I might be kinder than Brody, but I would be stupid to let you get away."

"How much longer are you going to keep me?"

"Until Brody says to let you go." He motions to the dresser with the water pitcher. "You got two minutes to wash your face and fix your hair like you women like to do."

"Don't I get a visit to the water closet, too?"

"You went last night. Two minutes." He puts his knife away and rests his hand on the butt of his gun.

I use the pitcher on the dresser and pour what's left of the water in the bowl. I splash it on my face and take a gander in the mirror. Lord, my hair! I unbraid it and it springs everywhere!

I take my time watching Emory in the mirror. "She's your wife, and she's ill. You should check on her."

"You should mind your business," he grumbles.

I run my fingers through my tangles, use some water to calm it down. Quickly, I work it back into a braid and it falls over my shoulder.

A knock comes on the door and Emory opens it. Jed Warner stands in the doorway, his face red and his eyes narrow in on me. Behind him, Minnie stands with her hands behind her back.

What's she got up her sleeve?

"So, it's true." Jed pushes Emory out of the way and stands in the middle of the room. "You've got a lot of nerve coming into my hotel."

"I told you he wouldn't like me being here," I said to Emory.

"What are you doing here?" Jed asks. "How did you get in

here?"

"I asked her." Emory keeps his hand on his gun.

Minnie's eyes widen.

"My wife is ailing. Mrs. Townes rode with us on the stage. Since her husband's out of town, she offered to stay with my Anabel while I took care of business in other parts of town."

Jed pulls up to his full height. He doesn't bother with a jacket, and his suspenders look like they are about to come loose. "Because of past events, Mrs. Townes has been banned from the Warner Hotel."

"Is that right? Must have been serious for a woman to not be allowed in a fine establishment like this." Leave it to Emory to put it on thick.

"When Mr. Warner said I wasn't welcome in his hotel to gain favor with a certain Miss Davenport, I didn't think he would take it this far. I saved Miss Davenport's life. Unfortunately, during that incident, Ms. Davenport fell down a flight of stairs and broke her leg. She blames me for her injury more than praise for saving her neck. Mr. Warner seems to echo her ungratefulness."

"Well, I know my Anabel is grateful for your company, Mrs. Townes." Then he turns to Jed Warner. "We were about to check on my wife. She hasn't returned from the water closet."

"Then, by all means," Jed steps aside. "I hope your wife is feeling better. Minnie, fetch Mrs. Fender some ginger tea while I escort Mrs. Townes out of my hotel."

"That won't be necessary. I can see myself out."

"I insist." Jed reaches for me, but Emory steps between us.

"Mrs. Townes will leave when my wife and I leave. If there is a problem with that, my wife and I will have to see about staying somewhere else. I believe there's a boarding house here in town?"

"Yes, I stay there most times while in town. It's a lovely

place, and the owner is much more friendly." My skin itches with nerves. I'm not about to allow any outlaws to threaten Ruby and risk having a run in with Sheriff Bentley while he recovers.

Warner presses his lips together in thought.

"We should check on Anabel," I say.

"Agreed," Emory picks up his hat. He gives me a look; a warning and I'm not sure Warner is smart enough to pick up on it. I turn and he catches my arm. "I think I left my hat on the stage."

"We'll see about it on our way to the cafe'. Anabel and I appreciate your company as we get familiar with town." He keeps saying it. Warner plucks at his suspenders, annoyed.

"Minnie will get you some tea, I'd offer for you to sit in the dining room, but given the circumstances," he looks at me and then back at Minnie. "Why are you still standing there? Go. Get Mrs. Fender some tea!"

Minnie turns and takes off down the hall.

"Don't worry about it. We've got an appointment and I believe Mrs. Fender would prefer the cafe. Shall we?" Emory presses on my back. "If you'll move out of our way, I need to check on my wife."

Emory narrows his eyes. He takes my arm and as we pass Jed Warner.

"Of course," Warner says. "I hope your wife is feeling better soon."

"Nothing nine months won't cure," I say with a smile. Warner seems relieved. After the food poisoning, some people in town experienced a few weeks back. I suppose it's good to know an epidemic has been avoided.

As we go to pass Warner, I say, "When you see Ms. Davenport, let her know I met her finance' a Mr. Charles Conway in Silver Valley. He mentioned concluding his business and being on the next stage. I've never seen a man happier to get to his bride than Mr. Conway. He spoke of her so highly." I put on my best lady-like voice like Daphne would and smile.

Warner's face turns another tint of red.

We head down the hall to the water closet. Emory knocks. "Anabel, love, you doing, okay?"

Hacking and wrenching noises come from the other side of the door. I hug myself and say a brief prayer for the woman. It sounds like she's having an awful time in there. "Is it always like this?"

"How would I know?" he grumbles.

"Anabel? You okay? You need anything?" I say through the door.

A minute later, the door opens. Anabel looks as white as a sheet. Her hair is tied back, and she leans against the doorway. "I think I need to go lay back down for a while. Maybe some tea and a biscuit until this passes."

"We don't got time for you to be laying down," Emory keeps the hall blocked off to eliminate any attempt for me to escape him. "We have to be at the bank by nine o'clock."

"You're going to have to go without me. I told you mornings aren't good for me." Her face blanches, and she turns away. I cover my mouth at the sounds of her heaving and my stomach moves with it. Maybe this pregnancy thing isn't as appealing as I first figured.

"Oh, not you too!" Emory grabs me. "Anabel, stay in the room. I'll be back when this is over."

He yanks me down the hall toward the steps.

Down in the lobby, Irwin Brownell steps out from around the corner. He put on his hat, looking much different from the outlaw drawing on the wanted poster. He wears a suit more dapper than the ones I have seen the gambler wear. As we approach, he checks his watch in his vest pocket. "Where is your wife?"

"She's not going to make it," Emory says. "We'll need to go

without her."

"What about the bank, man?" Irwin wears his gun, a long-barreled six-shooter, on his left hip. Few men are lefties.

"He'll have to deal with me or not at all. Not like Anabel can own land, anyway." Emory says.

"Right." Irwin takes a step closer to me. He offers his arm to me. "No sense in causing gossip about you walking around with another man's husband."

"Oh, but walking around with a single man is better?" I take his arm, not impressed with the girth. The bounty hunter has arms the size of small tree trunks. Irwin Brownell is a sapling compared to my husband.

"Grouchy in the morning, are we?"

"Only when in forced company," I quip. "I see you lost the uniform. Not a good look on you. Did you get a new haircut and a shave?" I ask.

He twitches his nose, a habit more than an irritant. I wonder if he'll grow his beard and mustache back when this is over. He'll have plenty of time in the Stoney Lonesome after I figure out how to put him there.

"Brody won't like this. Anything goes wrong and your wife won't have to worry about finding Ebbie's dead body."

Emory stomps his boots, taking the lead. With my hand on his arm, Irwin draws his gun as we go to walk out of the hotel.

A gasp comes from behind us, and I turn my head. Of all the times for Daphne Davenport to come down the stairs, she had to choose this one. She's got on a lavender gown and a crutch under one arm. Her raven locks are curled at the side of her face and her lips are puckered in disgust.

"I had to see it for myself. You couldn't stay away, even when you're told you're not welcome. How dare you! You have some nerve after trying to kill me. Did you think you could come and finish the job?" She stifles a sob. Curling a fist, she puts it against her mouth for a moment, then says, "Mr.

Warner said you'd come here. He also said he told you to leave. Go. Before I have to call on Sheriff Payne to arrest you!"

"Sheriff Payne?" I say in disbelief. "You mean Deputy. The bounty hunter is the sheriff. I watched Bently give him the star."

She sniffles. "You are not a nice woman, Jo Dee. See how she is out to humiliate me?"

I try not to roll my eyes at hearing her call me by that ridiculous pronunciation of my name. "Says the woman who could stand right in front of a bunch of outlaws and never know it," I say.

Irwin tightens his grip on my arm. "Time to go Mrs. Townes."

I grit my teeth against the pain.

"To think I tried to befriend you and help you. To see you now," Daphne presses her hand against her bust and lifts her chin. "You can't be happy unless you're always in the company of other men. You're no better than that woman who claims she's your mother."

Inside, what little respect I held for Daphne evaporates. Of all the things she could have said, she chose to insult me in the lowest way. There are a lot of things I'd like to say to her, but I won't. I can't. Not with two outlaws taking me who knows where for most likely the last time.

I do what Ruby always taught me. When you're mad and have nothing nice to say, don't say anything. So, I don't. Irwin pokes my ribs and we head for the door.

"You're not a good person. You'll never be a respected woman in this community!" Daphne screeches. I hear the crutch on the floor as she hobbles near us.

"You done? Because we need to go," I say, hoping Daphne does nothing else that might give these men reason to harm her or bring her along. I have no idea how I'm going to survive this, let alone to protect Daphne. Again.

Irwin pretends to be a gentleman. He waits as I glance back and Daphne hones those matching lavender eyes on me. "Mr. Warner said you saw Charles. I think you're lying."

"I did." I say, but one look at Irwin and I know we must go. "He looks much like his father in the face, more stout, but I recognized him, and he confirmed. I wish you both the best. I can see why your father would encourage the match."

Daphne fusses with a piece of lace on her bodice. "What did I ever do to you to have you hate me in such a way?"

Jed Warner comes down the stairs.

I shouldn't have, but I can't resist. She shouldn't have said those things and compared me to Polly. In a way, I'm doing Warner a favor.

"I would have thought you would be glad to marry a man like Charles Conway. He doesn't seem at all worried about your lack of dowry. With all your father has invested in his father's rail business, it's a match made in heaven."

Her eyes widen, her jaw unhinges and before she can make a noise, I say, "If you'll excuse me, I have business I must attend to before my husband, *the sheriff*, returns."

Before I can blink, Irwin has me outside on the walk. "You're a vicious woman, Mrs. Townes."

"She started it."

"Sounded like you did when you broke her leg," Emory says, putting on his hat.

"How was I supposed to know when I knocked her down the stairs to avoid a bullet, she'd break a leg?"

Irwin chuckled. "Yep, you're a spit fire compared to the last Mrs. Townes. If you weren't spoken for, I think I'd ask you to be my wife."

"You and someone else I know." I look toward the saloon in hopes the gambler will come strolling out. This early in the morning, he's probably fast asleep.

The tension of the morning gets to me. I roll back my

shoulders, trying to ease the discomfort. The more we walk, the more I feel as if someone is staring me right in the back.

Irwin must feel it, too. He pulls his gun from the holster and jabs it into my side. Outside the cafe' I spot Ford and down by the telegram office, I spot the stagecoach. "What's going on?"

Irwin doesn't speak. He glances behind us. Across from us, Deputy Payne steps out of the sheriff's office and, for a moment, I think he and Irwin know each other. He reaches into his vest, and I suck in a breath. The barrel of Irwin's gun shifts against me a second before I glimpse Chitto on the roof above the saloon. His rifle points toward the bank.

Emory opens the door to the bank, and we go inside. A few customers stand in line, but none of them look happy. The clerk looks at Emory, steps away and goes over to knock on Campbell Reed's door. We move closer to the bank manager's office as the clerk returns to a man who slams his fist down on the counter. "I can't pay my loan when my money got stole. How do you expect me to pay up in full? My loan isn't even due yet!" the stout farmer shouts, waving a paper in his hand.

"I'm sorry you'll need to speak with Mr. Reed. If you want to wait," the clerk says and points to the others standing against the wall.

"All these people are making me nervous," Irwin whispers.

The door opens, and Brody Brownell, not Campbell Reed, motions for us to come in. Reed sits behind his desk, his hands up. Brody has his gun out and the door slams shut as soon as we're through it.

"He's trying to go back on the deal," Brody waves his gun.

Startled to see me, Reed asks, "What is she doing here?"

"Because I say she is," Brody leans forward on the desk, his hands gripping the edge. His gun lies flat and points toward Reed. "Let's get the papers signed. Then we'll take care of the other matter."

"I've got your papers right here," Reed slides them in Emory's direction. "Where. Where is your wife?"

"Anabel couldn't make it. You don't need her to sign," Emory says.

Reed glances at Brody, sweat rolling down the man's jowls. "Does this mean you don't have the money?"

Brody looks back at Emory. "Where's Anabel?"

"She's sick. We should have waited until later, but we have a time schedule to keep," Emory says.

"That's not part of our deal." Reed pulls out a handkerchief and both Irwin and Emory point their weapons on him. His pudgy hands go straight up and seeing the handkerchief, the weapons lower, slightly. He pats the sweat on his head. "How do I know you'll come through with the money?"

"How do I know this here document gives me the right to the land you promised?" Emory steps up, signs the paper, and pushes the paper toward Reed again.

"You'll get your money like I said you would." Brody steps back at the sounds of shouts on the other side of the door.

"And what about her?" Reed says, "Surely you don't plan to kill her." He presses the cloth to his neck. "What if she tells that bounty hunter husband of hers?"

I lean a little and whisper in the same gruff voice as Mr. Reed, "That bounty hunter husband of mine is the sheriff, and he already knows these guys robbed your bank. What he doesn't know is why you're doing business with them."

Flustered, Reed scoots back. "These men are the robbers?"

I laugh, the nerves twisting and tingling inside me come out as I think of the irony of this all. Of course, Campbell Reed would be a part of this.

"You had me. Good one."

They all look at me as if I've grown two heads and I can't stop laughing. More shouts come from inside the bank.

"You had them rob the bank. You're calling in the loans on all the local's mortgages."

Before I can go further, someone pounds on the door. "Reed. Open up!"

My heart skips a beat. I know that voice.

Suddenly, I'm yanked from behind and Brody says, "See boys, this is why you always bring insurance when you come to the bank." His glee points in the center of my back. The cold steel presses against my spine.

"Is there another way out?" Emory asks.

"There's the window." Reed points. His hand shaking.

Emory heads for the window as the door bursts open. The bounty hunter has his gun out, Brody lifts to shoot and twist, making his aim off. The bounty hunter dives and scrambles to get behind Reed's desk. Emory dives out of the window. Irwin keeps his gun pointed at Reed.

"Shoot and your wife eats my bullets," Brody warns.

"What are you doing?" Irwin hisses. "This isn't part of the plan."

"Therefore, I had you bring insurance, brother. Payne said the sheriff was coming back."

"He's back." I say, knees knocking, and praying the bounty hunter doesn't kill me first for getting into the mess when he told me to steer clear.

Has it gotten chilly in here? Goosebumps race up my arms and I shiver against Brody Brownell. He keeps his gun pointed into my ribs, his arm hooks around my neck. Irwin points his gun at Reed, and the bounty hunter keeps his gun on Brody.

Outside the office, people run from the bank. A shot rings out from outside, causing more commotion. No one moves. I don't dare breathe.

Reed glances down at his desk, and something tells me his next move will determine which one of us dies first.

19

From the other side of the door someone yells, "Why do they get to go in there? We've been waiting?" Someone else says loudly, "If the sheriff is in here, then who is out there?"

The door flies back. It bounces off the wall as the farmer bursts into Reed's office. "Listen here, Reed—." He doesn't get to finish as the banker reaches inside his pocket.

Irwin's gun wavers between Reed and the farmer. He picks Reed and rushes toward him. The banker freezes. The farmer plows in, and the bounty hunter shouts for the others to stay out. Brody yanks me harder against him, and I stomp on his foot, trying to twist away. He slams me against the wall, gun no longer in my ribs. It clicks near my ear as he pulls the hammer back. "Nobody moves or she's dead." He presses me harder into the wall.

The side of my face sticks to the wallpaper. I stare at the bounty hunter waiting for him to make a move. Blinking to let him know it's okay whatever he decides to do. He grits his teeth, a growl slipping through. He holds his gun poised. The farmer holds out his hands to keep the others back.

Irwin motions for Reed and the portly banker moves toward him. He keeps his gun pointed at the banker's heart.

"He's part of it." I rush to tell the bounty hunter what may be my last words. "Reed's in on it."

"I am not," Reed bristles. "Would these men be threatening to kill me if I were?"

"Jo," the bounty hunter says.

"I'm not lying," I say and Brody laughs. "Let's go Irwin. Our business here is done."

"And how do you suppose on doing that?" the bounty hunter asks.

"The same way I came in." Brody eases the pressure off me against the wall. "With your wife."

"Leave her. Your issues are with me," the bounty hunter says.

"Ah, but I know better. As soon as I let her go, you'll shoot me in the back," Brody says. "Your reputation proceeds you, Townes."

"You're all a bunch of crooks," the farmer says. Irwin aims his gun at the man. Reed gives him a shove, and the gun goes off. I feel the heat whiz past my cheek. The farmer lounges forward and Brody's gun goes off next. I scream as Brody pulls me in front of him. The bounty hunter goes to fire, but he can't. I'm standing in his way. Brody shoves me out into the other part of the bank. He waves his gun and tells everyone to keep down. Inside the office, the bounty hunter bends to check on the farmer, who rolls over and groans. Brody drags me out of the bank.

Deputy Payne has his back towards us, his gun pointed toward the hotel.

"Payne!" I yell.

The man turns and looks at Brody. His gun drops and Brody threatens for no one to come near.

"You won't get away with this," I say.

"I am, and I will." Brody forces me down the street. The stagecoach comes our way. Ford Surles is the driver once more. As it slows, Chitto leaps atop it. He lands like a cat, holding onto the edges and crawling on the top. The door pops open and Brody lets go of me and jumps for inside. As he lands, he aims his gun towards me.

"Jolene!" I hear Polly, my mother, scream. Shots fire, and the world slows. Chitto takes the reigns of the stage, and Brody's gun flies from his hand. Payne stands there, his gun by his side, his eyes as wide as saucers, and my life flashes before my eyes.

I hit the boardwalk, a heavy body atop mine. All I can see is black. The world goes dark, and it's hard to breathe.

After several moments, I realize the body atop mine warms me. Hot breath blows on my neck, and I shove against the weight. Raising up on his arms, the bounty hunter looks down at me. "We've really got to stop doing this, Dimples," he says.

"Are you hurt?" I ask.

"No," he says, "You?"

"I'll live. But Brody and his gang are getting away!" I try to get out from beneath him. The bounty hunter gets to his feet, grunts, and holds out his hand to pull me up.

"He won't get far. Look." The bounty hunter nods as the rain picks up from a gentle mist to a steady pour. Down the street, Ford Surles falls from the coach and hits the mud. Chitto jumps down, rifle in hand, and hauls Ford to his feet. Behind him, the door opens to the stage and Brody comes stumbling out. Sheriff Silver hops out of the stage. "Where's Irwin and Emory?" My heart races.

"Emory Fender aka McLoughlin is behind bars." Deputy Payne walks up to us. "I would have had one of the Brownell brothers if it weren't for your wife getting in the way," Payne puts his gun back in the holster. I doubt the man ever fired it.

Out from the side of the bank, a horse and rider take off in the opposite direction. Chitto aims his rifle, and several shots go off, but none takes down the outlaw.

"Shouldn't you go after him?" asks Payne.

The bounty hunter slings his arm around my shoulders. "Let him go."

I turn to look at my husband and frown. He's got a bead of sweat on his forehead. "You're gonna let Irwin get away?"

"Head start," the bounty hunter says. "He won't get far."

"And neither will you," I spot the red bleeding into his shirt from his shoulder to his chest. "Chord." Panic rises from within me. "Chord, you're bleeding."

"If I'd known a nick and some blood would get you to say my name, Dimples, I would have got shot sooner."

"Shot. Oh God, please no." I push at his jacket, see the blooming stain and he stops me.

"Jo."

"Don't you dare die on me, bounty hunter."

He wraps his arms around me and leans his forehead against me. "It nicked the top of my shoulder, Jo. You can't get rid of me that easy."

"I thought you wanted to get rid of me," I breathe. "I didn't think you wanted a second wife, let alone one like me."

He cups my face and a bunch of knots form in my stomach. "I'm a man of my word and we still have a deal."

"We still have a deal," I echo his words.

He smiles, not something he does often, and I tilt my face up, his lips brush against mine, glide over my cheek, and he whispers. "Let's get me some stitches, a fresh shirt, and some pie."

Inside the doctor's office, I helped slip off the bounty hunter's long jacket. With his shoulder bleeding, it makes little sense to have him moving his arm. I do what any good wife does. I help him remove his shirt. One button at a time. My fingers going numb, my teeth sinking into my bottom lip, a bit of sweat rolls down my neck. "I can get it if you're having trouble."

"Nope. I got it." I keep my eyes on the buttons, each one opening more and more of my husband's bare chest. Swallowing hard, I tackle the last one. The bounty hunter hisses as the doctor pulls it down off his wounded shoulder. Soon his shirt is in my hands, and I look anywhere but at the open expanse of his chest. I've seen men's bare chests plenty of times when visiting Chitto and his tribe. There's nothing a girl should get embarrassed about. However, seeing the bounty hunter exposed causes more sweat beneath the sisters. As I turn away, the bounty hunter grabs my hand. "It'll be okay."

The way he says it, the sound of his teeth gritting makes me look his way. I can see the pain in his eyes.

"I'm sorry about what Brody did to your wife."

His fist clenches as the doctor makes him sit down. Mrs. Chierhart comes to his aid with water and clothes to clean the bounty hunter's broad shoulder.

Feeling sick, not from the sight of blood so much as the aftermath of what happened, I say, "I'm sorry I put you in danger." The feeling builds and I take deep breaths, trying to contain it. Soon I fear the world will spin.

"Jo," The bounty hunter squeezes my hand, enough to get my attention, but not to hurt me.

I shake my head.

"What did Brody tell you?" The bounty hunter hisses as Doc Chierhart goes to work on stitching his shoulder.

"Just a deep graze," Mrs. Chierhart says for my benefit. "Gonna be fine. Need more stitches to repair the shirt, I figure."

It's not the bounty hunter's shirt I'm worried about. I clutch it in my free hand with his jacket over the same arm.

"You'll want to wash it right away, get the stain out. You can wash it here," Mrs. Chierhart says to distract me.

"I'm sure the bounty hunter wants to put it back on before we go. I can wash it when we get to Ruby's. You have a clean one there in our room, don't you?"

"We're back to 'the bounty hunter'," Chord inhales and lets his breath out slowly between his teeth. "It's over Jo. You don't have to be scared. Whatever Brody told you; he lies."

"I'm not scared." I look him in those stone-colored eyes, as gray as the sky outside. Three times now I've almost gotten killed, nearly gotten someone else killed or hurt.

"Here, why don't you sit?" Mrs. Chierhart reaches for the bounty hunter's jacket. I keep his shirt and let go of his hand. "I should take this to Ruby and get it washed. I'll fetch you a clean one."

"You don't need to do that, Dimples. Doc is almost done. We can walk to Ruby's together."

"No. You stay here with the doctor and let him fix you up. I'll run to Ruby's. It won't take long, and then we can go have that pie."

The bounty hunter looks at me beseechingly. It near cuts me to the knees and makes me stumble to get out of there. He grunts as the doctor works on his shoulder. Mrs. Chierhart offers him a drink to take the edge of the pain. She keeps swiping at the blood while the doctor makes neat little stitches. My stomach rolls and pitches as I stand there. I have to go. Breathing doesn't help. The walls are getting closer in the small room, and I take off with Chord's shirt in my hands.

Halfway back to Ruby's, I spot Mrs. McLoughlin stepping out of the hotel. She seems lost and pats down her skirts. Under my palm, something digs in through the fabric. I sort through the shirt until I get to the pocket. Inside it, Anabel's wedding ring falls out in my hand.

The bounty hunter forgot to place it in the safe with the sheriff in Silver Valley. Fisting the gold band, I head in Anabel's direction. She pulls out a parcel ready to step into the rain when I call out her name. She turns and looks as I hold up my fist. At the same moment, I run right smack into the gambler. Those emerald eyes light up as they spot me.

I drop the shirt to hold on to the ring. It goes straight down into the mud. "Now look what you made me do."

"Let me help you, Darlin'."

A wagon comes down the street, slouching mud in our direction and burying the bounty hunter's shirt. Great, one more stain I need to scrub out.

Fetching the muddy garment, I grimace. The gambler looks at me and grins. "I've missed you. Have I told you that?"

"Can't see how you have," I say, stomping away in Anabel's direction. She stands, her face paler by the minute. Stepping back, I'm afraid she'll run, and I take off after her. "Wait! I have something for you!"

The closer I get to the hotel, I notice Daphne stepping out with her crutch. She turns her back, but not before sticking out her wooden crutch as I go past. Tripping, I grab her as I go down. This time I'm on the bottom and she's howling like a caged coyote. The ring slips from my fingers, goes rolling down the board. It spins and curves to the right. Holding my breath, I watch as it lands at Anabel's feet.

"Oh, my goodness. Are you okay?" Anabel goes to step forward and I shout. "Stop!"

I shove Daphne off, scramble for the ring and hold it up. "I believe this is yours."

"Is that my wedding ring?" Anabel reaches for it. She turns it and slips it on her finger. "I thought I lost it for good." She whispers. "You know I was so mad, and now it doesn't seem to matter." Tears well in her eyes.

"You… You…" Daphne sputters as the gambler helps her to her feet. Mud smears the side of her lavender gown. "Did you see what she did to me?"

"I sure did." Anabel isn't looking at Daphne, though. She's looking at the ring on her finger. Her gaze lifts, and she says, "Emory's dead. They shot him trying to escape the bank."

"Deputy Payne said he arrested him and put him in jail," I say.

Tears brim in Anabel's eyes. "It was that Indian man. He captured Ford, too, and took him to jail."

My heart goes out to Anabel. Somehow, this news doesn't surprise me. I figured Payne had a part in this. Why lie and say he put Emory in jail?

Daphne walks over about to grab hold of me when the gambler says, "Miss Davenport, I believe you forgot your crutch."

We all look and there Daphne stands on both feet. She cries out and reaches for it.

"What have you done now?" Mr. Warner walks out and points his finger at me.

"Miss Davenport no longer needs her crutch," I say.

He looks her up, and down, glances at the gambler, then nods. Turning his attention to Anabel, he says, "The Sheriff from Silver Valley is looking for you, Ms. Fender. He asked I detain you here until he can seek you out. Would you like to come back inside? I'll have tea made and you can stay out of this rain."

"I suppose it would do me no good to avoid him, now would it?" She pulls down her parcel and closes it. "My other business can wait." Then she takes my hand in hers. "I'm truly sorry for all you've been through. Emory was doing what he thought was best for our family. Doesn't seem worth it now."

She frowns, her chin wobbling as more tears escape from her eyes. "I am gonna be okay, you know. I got the boys and we've got our land. Emory signed the papers, didn't he?"

I don't have the heart to tell her those papers aren't legal and the money she and Emory deposited in the bank belongs to the people of Deadwood.

"I'm sure Sheriff Silver will help straighten everything out, along with my husband, when he's able. Be sure to tell him the truth," I say.

"Please, tell me. I need to know. What really happened to Ebbie?"

"He's dead, Anabel. I found him along the road. Well, Chitto, the Indian man, found him. Someone shot him and took his horse. His body is out at an old cabin outside of Silver Valley. The sheriff gave me ten dollars to bury him." I reach in my skirt pocket and notice the way Anabel's seem lumpy rather than wrinkled.

"This is what I got left," I offer her the money.

She takes the money, her nose turning red and more water flows from her eyes than the stream forming in the roads from all the rain. I'm gonna be soaked by the time I get to Ruby's.

"Come now, Ms. McLoughlin, Let me escort you inside." Mr. Warner takes her parcel as she reaches to lift her skirts. "You may want to dry out your skirts inside. I'd hate for all that money to fall apart because it got wet."

Her jaw unhinges.

Warner frowns so deep his brows touch each other between his eyes.

"You might want to help her with that for when the sheriff comes. If I had to guess right, she's carrying at least half the town's savings in those pleats."

Anabel scowls at me. The gambler offers to go find the Sheriff. I tell him the bounty hunter is at the doctor's place and I'm headed to Ruby's, where I hope the former sheriff Bentley is alive and well. "Sheriff Silver is locking up the felons at the jail, and Payne is watching over them until this mess is sorted out."

"Payne?" I grab the gambler's arm. "When you go find Sheriff Silver, you tell him the good deputy of Deadwood can't be trusted. I saw him and Brody Brownell having a conversation weeks back. Then today he let Brody go right by him. Oh, and he lied about putting Emory McLoughlin in jail."

"That's a whole lot of accusations. Are you sure, darlin'?" The gambler asks.

"I wouldn't say it if it wasn't true." I look at Anabel, who avoids my gaze. She tries to back up, but Warner takes her arm. "This way Ms. Fender."

The gambler heads one way and Warner helps Ms. Fender McLoughlin into the hotel. Daphne bunches her skirts into her hands. "What about me?"

"You're standing right by the door. Don't tell me you were going out in this weather. It might ruin your curls." I take off, not caring about the rain. All I want to do is reach Ruby's, grab the bounty hunter a new shirt, and hope my legs don't give out by the time I get there. Getting kidnapped, almost killed, and watching the bounty hunter get hurt can sap the energy right out of a girl.

Looking down at the muddy shirt, I can't help thinking what a mess I've made of things. By the time I reach Ruby's, she's standing there waiting for me with a blanket, as if she knew I would walk through that door any moment. And as I allow her to wrap me in its warmth and her arms, the damn burst and the tears let go. "I can't stay. I need to get the bounty hunter a new shirt."

"Robbie," Ruby calls. "Fetch Chord a shirt and take it to him."

"He's at the doctor's place," I manage to say. "I told him I'd be back, and we'd get pie."

"Then it's a good thing I baked this morning. Come now, you've had a long trip getting back here, and there's no need going back out there in the storm."

I know better to argue with Ruby. She leads me into the living room. The former sheriff leans back on the couch, a sling around his arm, and his worry as palatable as mine.

20

Later in the evening, the bounty hunter returns to the boarding house where we more or less live. The bounty hunter pays Ruby a monthly rate for always keeping a room for him — a room I now occupy as his wife.

With the rain still coming down and the candles lit in the living room, the bounty hunter fills the former sheriff of Deadwood in on our little adventure. Normally, I'd add my two cents, but instead I serve him a piece of Ruby's apple pie. The bounty hunter's expression softens as he looks at me. A ripple of pleasure flows through me as I head to our room, alone.

For a while, I watch the rain race down the window in streams, but it's enough the bounty hunter lives. I think of Anabel and hearing the bounty hunter say they recovered another chunk of the town's money in the stage and her skirt.

A deep chill settles in my bones as I crawl between the blankets. I can't seem to get warm enough. Ruby warned me sometimes when I person's been through as much as I have in a day, their bones need to rest. I kick off my cowgirl boots and curl up, shivering, and praying I'm not wrong. I know what I heard, but I wonder if the bounty hunter believes me about Campbell Reed.

For now, one Brownell is in jail, and the other has escaped. I say an extra prayer for Anabel Fender McLoughlin. She has family to raise her children while she checks in at the Gray Bar Hotel. According to the bounty hunter, she came clean with Sheriff Silver. She even gave him the rest of the ten dollars I'd given her to bury her brother's body.

Robbie, Amaryllis's son from the saloon, got the bounty hunter his shirt and on the way back, he met with Sheriff Silver at the hotel. He left Chitto with Sheriff Silver and Deputy Payne to watch the prisoner, Brody Brownell. I heard the bounty hunter confess to setting this all up with Sheriff Silver to catch the Brownell gang. The one part they hadn't counted on was me. Silver put me in jail to keep me safe. He knew Chitto would go with Ford. They'd planned it ahead. Throwing me on the stage was a last-minute decision by Silver. The bounty admitted he didn't like that part of the plan, but I'd already gotten in too deep for him to safely capture the outlaws and keep me safe.

I heard him admit to Bentely he didn't want another wife. "She keeps getting in the way. I can't do my job and babysit a woman who doesn't have enough sense to stay home."

With my heart, body, and mind aching, I decide to stay in bed as long as it takes to feel warm and wanted again.

The rain goes on forever. Twice Chitto comes to visit me. He, too, waits in the rain. He and Sheriff Silver will take Ford and Anabel back to Silver Valley, where they'll get a trail. Brody will stay in Deadwood. The bounty hunter sent a telegram to the rangers who will send a special escort for the outlaw. Something tells me Brody Brownell's final destination comes with a noose. No one confessed outright to killing Buck Dawson, and two of the robbers are dead. It's for the judge to decide, but Ford Surles has killed a few men and around here there's no life in prison. We hang people for stealing horses. Taking a life is a much more serious offense. Dakota Territory might modernize with the railroad, but we're still west of the eastern civilization.

For days, I watch the rain run down the window in my room. Ruby brings tea and tries to bribe me from my bed.

The bounty hunter avoids me.

Twice now, I've ventured downstairs. Ruby and I have baked apple pies, and neither day had we seen hide or hair of my husband.

The streets are filling with so much water it has delayed Sheriff Silver and Chitto from leaving town. Almost a week goes by and the chill stays in my bones. I got a runny nose and a cough, but a little honey in my tea has kept it at bay. It's the weather according to the doctor who came to check on Bentely and Ruby insisted I see.

When the sun comes out for a small period, Chitto finds me in the sitting room, curled up with a blanket. "I'm going to Silver Valley with the Sheriff. "

"Who will watch over the deputy? I mean, help watch the prisoner? Bentely still hasn't healed enough to return to his duties."

"Man Hunter has been staying nights at the jail. He has vowed to the man, Brody Brownell, to see him hang. The other, Payne, he disappeared a few nights ago."

"Any ideas?"

"Some say he go after the other brother on his own. Hard to tell."

"Where will you go after Silver Valley?"

"From there, I will get my horse and return to the mountain. *Pavati* will worry if I do not return soon. She grows heavier with child. Our little one comes before the leaves change."

I lean my head back, give him a good long look and sigh. "I

would ask to go with you, but with this cold and the weather, and without my pony, I don't think I would make it."

Chitto frowns. He sits on the floor near my feet. I've got on thick wool socks and a wool skirt despite it being August. He places his hand on my knee. "Something more ails you."

"I want to go home," I tell him with a heavy heart. "I don't belong here. I'm not made to live in a place like this."

Chitto nods.

"Yellow Cat came looking for you."

"You understand. I must go."

"It's safer for you in the mountains." And me too, but I don't let it pass my lips.

"Man Hunter. He does not make you happy?"

I don't answer.

Chitto makes a face. One where I know he has made a decision not even he agrees with but will do it, anyway. Which is why when he says, "I will go with the sheriff to Silver Valley. Once the prisoners are secure, I will get my horse and come here first for you. By then, you should be well to ride?"

"No." I put my hand over his. "*Pavati*, Clear Brook, waits for you. Do not miss out on your child's birth. Your wife needs you."

Chitto places his other hand and traps mine. "You, Willow, are also my wife. I give you to Man Hunter, but if he does not care for you in the ways a man should his woman, I take you back. You are not happy here. The tribe is your family."

"I am her family."

We both look up. The bounty hunter stands in the door-way. He wears a new tan shirt with his sheriff's star pinned on the pocket. His six -shooter is strapped to his hip and his long jacket is missing. He has his hat in his hands and his dark hair tied back. The strong angles of his face crease folding his brow.

Chitto raises to his feet. He ditched the Calvary uniform and wears his buckskins. His rifle leans against the doorway.

The bounty hunter picks it up and holds it out to Chitto. "We can take it out on the street if you want, but Jo's my wife and she stays here."

It loosens something in my chest. I don't know why, but hearing him say those words pleases me.

"You swore you would take care of her."

"And I am a man of word," the bounty hunter says.

"She is not happy here with you." Chitto takes his rifle.

"I think I know how to make her happy." The bounty hunter walks past Chitto. He crouches down, hanging his hat on his knee. He reaches into his pocket and pulls out a simple ring. Taking my hand slowly, he slips the wedding band onto my finger. "This belongs to no one but you, Dimples."

Words escape me, and tears tumble down. I can't seem to hold them in. When it rains, it pours around here. "You told Bentely that night you were shot you didn't want a wife. It's not like you asked me, and the judge slammed his gavel and made it so."

"I knew that morning I was going to marry you. First thing you should learn about me is… well, first," his expression softened, "You really do need to call me by my given name. It's Chord. And second, no one makes me do what I don't want to do."

"You still going to hand me over to another man when I find one willing to marry me? The gambler offered me a white picket fence and a couple of babies."

"Is that what you want?"

"No," I confess. "Well, maybe."

"I can't be that man."

"I know," I whisper, not wanting him to let go.

"We had a deal, and you broke it."

I shake my head, not knowing what he's talking about.

"Brody told you things. He said you asked."

Again, I shake my head.

"We'll need to talk about what happens when my wife doesn't keep her word."

"I'm sorry," I whisper.

"Not sorrier than I," he says, then looks at Chitto. "You mind if I have some privacy with my wife?"

Chitto takes his rifle and steps out of the room.

All that joy starts to deflate until he says, "All you need to know, Jo, is Brody Brownell killed my wife out of revenge against me for something I did. I didn't want another wife because I can't live through losing another one. I heard you tell Chitto you wanted to go back to the mountains. I can't let you do that either. I can't let you go knowing you'd become another man's wife."

"I'm nothing but trouble. You almost got killed this time because of me."

"And I've had to save you more times than I can count, but don't think for a moment I'm letting you take that ring off your finger."

The bounty hunter stood, placed his hat on my head, and pulled me from the chair. With the blanket still wrapped around my shoulders, the bounty hunter heists me up and I'm no small girl.

"What are you doing?"

"Something I should have done a long time ago."

The rain never stops and the puddles in the street grew larger. Sheriff Silver decides he can't wait any longer to get back to Silver Valley with his prisoners and take care of his town. Chitto drives the stagecoach. The stage company sent a man to take over once they reach Silver Valley. Sheriff Silver stays inside the coach where it's dry and to keep both Ford and Anabel from escaping. I don't think he'll have any trouble with

Anabel. She appeared a little green as she got inside, and my heart grows heavier for her. I shouldn't feel guilty or bad for the woman, but I do. All she wanted was a better life for her family and because of the way she went about trying to get it, the woman lost both her brother and her husband. Now her boys will have to live a few years without her. I think of the baby she's carrying. Pressing a hand to my stomach, I wonder again what it would be like.

I don't have any right thinking about babies and motherhood. The thought itself startles me. My own mother didn't leave the best impression on me, and what kind of mother would I make? But it makes me smile, and a little tickled at the same time. I press my hands to my warming cheeks as I think about how it could be a real possibility.

I wave as Chitto goes off on the stagecoach. He's wearing a hat and slicker to fend off the rain like the other man. Neither seemed happy of going off in this rain. I pray they don't run into any trouble on the way.

As I stand there outside the sheriff's office, a hand slips around my waist and pulls me back against the hard chest of the bounty hunter. He smells more like apple pie and cinnamon than his usual sweet tobacco. Ruby's been doing a lot of baking at the boarding house, staying inside, and caring for Bentely, who seems content to let her fuss over him.

But today, Bentely sits in his old seat behind the desk. He's got his arm tied up, and he's not as pale as the last couple of days. Bentely insists with Payne gone; he needs to help Chord keep an eye on the prisoner. That's right, Chord, not 'the bounty hunter,' seeing as he insists, I call him by his first name. He made sure I understood I'm his wife, and pleasant little zings tingle through my body remembering those private moments alone.

With his arm still around me, and Brody Brownell snoozing behind bars, Chord reaches up on his shirt and pulls his sheriff's star off. He holds it out to Bentley, "I'll be returning this to you."

Brody sits up from his cell cot and leans back with arms crossed. Unlike the Silver Valley sheriff's office, the Deadwood jail doesn't keep a wall between the cells and the sheriff. He likes them where he can see them at all times. With prisoners like Brody or even Ford, I can see why.

Bentely shakes his head. "You keep it, Chord. This old man isn't ready to go back in service full time." He taps the area on his chest where he got shot during the bank robbery weeks ago. "Besides, I'm here to help keep watch over the prisoner until they send the rangers to handle this one. Consider me a deputy for now."

A look exchanges between my husband and the former sheriff. I lay my hand on Chord's arm. "Do you really think Payne went after Irwin Brownell?"

Brody smirks from inside his cell.

"After all his big talk in town and making people believe he was sheriff, I'd say the man's out to prove himself," Bentley offers.

"It's hard to say," Chord scratches his chin.

"I wouldn't trust him," I say.

"You don't seem to trust many people these days." Bentley keeps his gun on the desk where it's easier to grab if he needs it. "You'd be right not to either. Not many folk you should," he says.

There are a couple of people I can think of I trust. Ella Mae, Ruby, Ella Mae's mother Pearl, and my husband, Chord.

"You should run along Dimples. A man needs to do his job." Chord slips his hand away from me.

Brody leans forward and I try to ignore him. Bentley looks content back in his old seat. "Maybe you should let Sheriff Bentley handle this. Brody's behind bars. He's not going anywhere."

"I'll see you out." Chord directs me to the door. Out under the porch roof, with rain drizzling down, he pulls me into his arms. "What is it, Dimples? I can see that mind of yours working."

"I don't have a good feeling about this. You should let Bentley handle Brody. I know he's healing from his injury, but Brody's in a cell. Bentley can still shoot if he tries to escape. You and Brody have a history and I don't want you veering off into a vengeful path. You can't let him goad you or do anything outside of being a sheriff now that you're wearing that star." I never got details about the past and I'm better off for not knowing. There's more to the secrets my husband holds from his past. His dead first wife, only one of them.

"Don't you worry, Dimples, I know the law."

That's what makes me afraid. "Promise me you won't kill him before the rangers come."

"I'm not going to kill him. Trust me, killing him would be far more merciful than what the Calvary will do when they catch up with a murdering, thieving, traitor."

I lay my hand on his chest. "Good, because you still need to arrest Campbell Reed."

"I can't arrest a man if he hasn't broken the law."

"He confessed while I was in with the outlaws. I told you, he's in on the robbery and stealing everyone's land."

Chord dips his chin in, "There's no law for the bank calling in loans. Most of the money has been returned and I've seen the accounts myself where it's being distributed evenly between all the accounts. Not everyone might have got all their money back, but it's better than broke."

"Don't you think it's curious? I saw Reed talking with Mr. Harritt behind the stables last month, remember? Then Payne tells everyone he's sheriff while you're gone, and Bentely's bed ridden. Those robbers came back to Deadwood because Brody had a silent partner. I heard it from them myself. This wasn't

Brody's idea, it was someone else's, and that someone else was Campbell Reed."

"Reed got shot during the robbery."

"So, he got stuck in the crossfire," I say, feeling frustrated.

"Then he's calling in loans, and that old couple staying at Ruby's a few weeks ago said they sold their claim on the mountain. Reed's up to something."

Chord places his hands on both my arms. "I believe you. Something's going on, but hearsay isn't proof. We have to catch him in the act or have more than one person willing to testify. If Brody or Irwin would speak against him, that is something, but they're already walking down dead man's row. It doesn't add up, either."

I tighten my lips.

We walk toward the bank. People are peering at the window, and Chord takes me inside. Mr. Davenport has his cane in the air as the clerk backs away. Reed steps out of his office and Chord asks, "Is there a problem here?"

"I tell you what the problem is." Davenport pauses to take a long look at me, then continues. "With the money returned, not ALL of us have received our accounts back in full!"

"Some customers have larger accounts than others. I assure you everyone has received back the same percentage to their accounts in order to make it fair," Reed talks to Chord, ignoring the rest of us.

"What about the rest of our money?" Davenport blusters.

"My father always taught me not to keep all my stash buried in one jar. You being a man of investing, I would have thought, would have things spread out," I say.

Davenport grunts, ignoring me. He says to Reed, "How do you expect the railroad to hold an account with you if you can't be trusted to keep the money safe?"

"I assure you; the bank is taking all necessary actions to prevent any further damage to our customer's accounts," Reed rocks back on his heels. "Since the law in this town doesn't seem to be reliable, I've hired my own man to oversee security here at the bank."

Deputy Liam Payne steps out from the corner.

Chord and I exchange a glance.

Davenport snorts. My sentiments, exactly.

Payne hands over his deputy star, claiming he doesn't need it. He rests his hand on his gun.

Back outside in the drizzling rain, I yearn for my hat. I glance at Chord, who says, "Don't say it."

"Fine." But with Payne working for Reed and Irwin on the loose, we're going to need more than the Calvary and a few Texas Rangers on the way to keep Deadwood a safe place for folks to settle.

That is, if they don't drown first.

It doesn't seem like it will ever stop raining.

WHAT'S NEXT?

Just when Jo thought she'd gotten her man, he disappears. The entire town is up in arms over electing a new sheriff after a notorious outlaw escapes. But where is the bounty hunter when you need him?

The Cowgirl Saves The Sheriff
Book 4

SNEAK PEEK

The Cowgirl Saves the Sheriff

For the several days, it's been eating my insides right out every time I see Ms. Daphne Davenport sitting inside the hotel dining room with Hannah Baker and Grace Adler. She hasn't looked at me since I revealed her penniless state and her fiance' on his way to Deadwood to claim his bride.

Except, I lied.

I haven't been able to sleep for several nights. Ruby patted me on the shoulder, thinking it's because Chord, the bounty hunter turned sheriff, has been spending nights at the jail to watch over an outlaw named Brody Brownell.

In all honestly, every time I see or hear the name Davenport or Conway, my gut twists as if I'm getting eaten from the inside out.

This miserable rain has everyone in Deadwood in a foul mood. Some women in town have taken to their sewing circles, baking, or trying to do up as many preserves as they have for canning while they can't do anything but stay inside. It's worse than winter. It's wet, cold, and miserable for the month of August.

On my way to take Chord a sandwich and a piece of pie, I spot Daphne in the dress shop. She's standing on a stool as Lottie fits her for a new dress. It's a pale yellow, softer than butter, and looks real nice with her black hair. Not too long ago, Lottie made me two new riding skirts and the blouse I'm wearing, thanks to the bounty hunter. I love my split skirt for going riding on my paint pony Lulu. Not that I've been riding her much since Chord brought her back to town.

What a debacle that was!

Brody and his gang robbed the bank and then tried to come back to town and buy land with the stolen money.

The Calvary can't get here soon enough to take Brody off the sheriff's hands. Chord and Brody have a history, one my husband made a deal with me to keep from trying to find out. All I know is Brody killed Chord's first wife. Why? I'm certain he did it for revenge.

While Chord and I know each other as intimately as a husband and wife should, there are still invisible walls between us. Something a wife shouldn't press to know, but I'm certain with Brody Brownell sitting in the jail every day reminding of the past, nothing good is going to come our way.

Inside the sheriff's office, Miles Clark stands while Chord reads from a piece of paper. He tucks it in his shirt pocket. "Good to know. I appreciate you bringing this by."

Miles has an accent to make every woman in Deadwood swoon when he talks. He tips his hat my way and heads out of the office. He lives at Ruby's boarding house along with Chord and I. Soon, Miles will sleep above the rail station if the rain ever lets up enough for them to finish building it. Until then, he's spent many a rainy evening in the boarding house sitting room with a cup of tea entertaining some ladies currently boarding at Ruby's. She's had an increase in female boarders since Miles arrived.

"Anything interesting?" I ask.

"The Calvary sent an update. They're close by," Chord says, glancing over his shoulder at Brody. The man lies on his cot staring up at the ceiling. "Must not be too close," the prisoner says. "Not that I'll be here when they come."

"You keep saying that." Chord takes the sack from me and pulls out his sandwich. "You know, you don't have to keep baking me pies," he says.

"You got a slice for me in there, *Mrs. Townes*," Brody asks.

The way he says my name causes goosebumps to race down my arms. Ignoring him, I take a seat across from the sheriff's desk and Chord sits on the corner.

"You like pie," I say.

"So do you." Chord winks and my cheeks warm to betray me. There's not much else to do at Ruby's. Besides helping her with the guests and keeping the chickens from drowning, what's a girl to do?

"That'll be the last of the apple," I tell him. "Won't be much more of anything if the rain doesn't stop and the crops keep getting flooded."

"Don't you know," Brody says from behind bars, "That there is heaven weeping. Once I'm out, the skies will clear and the sun will shine again, you'll see."

"That's enough Brody," Chord says.

"When's the Calvary say they'll be here?' Brody asks.

"Soon." Chord keeps his back to Brody.

"You'd be wise to let me go."

Chord shakes his head.

I glance over at Brody. Not long ago, he held a gun against me. Slight shivers rack over my body. Chord frowns. "You should have worn your jacket."

"I'm not cold."

By the look on his face, he can tell I'm lying, but I'm really not. Coming to the jail gives me all kinds of mixed emotions.

"She's easy on the eyes. Pity something happens to her because you couldn't do the right thing," Brody taunts.

"I think you should go," Chord gets off the desk, takes me by the arm and steers me out of the office.

"I don't like you here alone with him." I plant my feet to keep Chord from pushing me out.

"Bentely will come in a while and I've got a few things to look into, then I'll be home for a while or until supper."

He says it like we're this sweet little old married couple, not that we live in a boarding house and my husband hunts men for a living.

"Better enjoy it," Brody grins. "Might be your last."

"Are you threatening me?" My heart pounds in my chest. He killed the first Mrs. Townes. What will stop him from killing the second?

Chord holds open the door. "He's not going to come near you, Dimples."

At first I hated the nickname the bounty hunter gave me, but since we've been getting to know each other in a more intimate way, I don't mind it much. It sends pleasant little zings in my tummy.

"You don't know that, Chord. He could break out." I grip him. "He could kill you." I lean around my husband. "And if anything happens to you, he better run, because he won't make it out of Dakota Territory if I chase him."

Chord chuckles. "I believe you tried that once." His forehead touches mine. "He's not going to kill me, and he's not coming after you," he murmurs.

"Then what's all this talk?" My throat tightens. I lost my father a few months ago and my childhood crush, Chitto, went back to his tribe in the mountains, leaving me here with Chord and Ruby. Along with my best friend, Ella Mae, they've become my family. There's nothing in the world I wouldn't do to make sure nothing happens to them. Which is why I've been a good little wife and stayed at the boarding house helping Ruby and bringing Chord meals. I've put him in danger too many times, and it scares me. I can't lose one more person.

"Pay him no mind, Jo. He's blowing off steam and trying to upset you."

He's doing a good job of it from my perspective. The sheriff puts a finger under my chin. "Maybe instead of pie you can try fixing my shirt?"

During the shot out that led to Brody's capture, the bounty hunter got wounded in the shoulder. I said I would stitch his shirt and fix it, but then I dropped it in the mud and the stains didn't come out. Jensen's don't have any new ones with the lack of supplies coming in because of the weather and the railroad workers intercepting the deliveries in the mountains.

"I suppose I should." Or make him a fresh shirt, which is on my list to do, right after trying to prove Campbell Reed had something to do with the robbery last month.

"That's my girl," Chord grins.

"You'd best kiss her goodbye," Brody calls, "Might be the last time you see him."

Grabbing hold of Chord's shirt, my chest tightens. Chord places his hands over mine. "Shut it, Brody."

I kiss him anyway, shutting up Chord and pouring all my feelings into it. We haven't said anything about the 'L' word. Neither one of us say much about feelings. My bounty hunter, sheriff, husband isn't a man of many words, but I don't need words to tell me what these lips are saying to my heart.

Brody whistles and we pull apart.

Chord clears his throat, sends a death glare in Brody's direction. I take my cue and leave.

"Hey Jo?"

I turn back. "Wear your green dress tonight. We'll eat at the diner tonight."

Pressing my fingers against my lips, a wave of warmth wards away the chill in my bones. "I'll tell Ruby so she doesn't go setting places for us."

ABOUT THE AUTHOR

Growing up on a farm in Pennsylvania, Susan Lower yearned for adventure. A woodsy gal, Susan prefers camping over going to the beach any day. Still a farm girl at heart, Susan writes fast action reads filled with cowboys, heroes, and hope. She writes both western historical and contemporary romances, romantic suspense, and has been itching to one day write a mystery or thriller. Christmas is her favorite holiday, and she loves to write resilient characters struggling to overcome the complications of life while holding their values and strengthening their faith.

ALSO BY SUSAN LOWER

Silver Wind Equine Rescue Series

Love horses, cowboys, and second chances? The Silver Wind Horse Rescue series has both! While the members of the Silver Wind Horse Rescue set out to provide refuge for abused and abandoned horses, those very horses may be the salvation they need to find a second chance at love.

Forgotten Reins

Unbridled

Silver Stirrups

Hearts of Hidden Hills

Sweet and wholesome small town love stories filled with second chances and healing families provide a wonderful, feel-good read.

Residence of Her Heart

Salvaged Hearts

Reckless Hearts

Brides of Annie's Creek

Travel back to the old west where these women take love into their own hands and learn somethings can't be rushed.

Fruit Cake Bride

Thimble Bride

Postage Stamp Bride